THE

BREATH

BEFORE

FOREVER

THE BEAST
OF
MOSCOW
4

BETHANY-KRIS

Published by Bethany-Kris

www.bethanykris.com

ISBN 13: 978-1-989658-56-7

Editor: Elizabeth Peters

Cover Design © Bethany-Kris

For every woman who loves a beast.

CONTENTS

1.

"Happy birthday, to you. Happy birthday, to you."

One wouldn't think Vaslav Pashkov was the type of man to serenade his wife on her wedding night— even if that night also happened to be her birthday. Yet, he did exactly that, crooning happy birthday softly to Vera, and out of earshot of the scattered, few people that remained in the sitting room.

Mira promised Vera a wedding dinner worthy of celebration with her family and friend and delivered. After everything had been said and done, and the plates cleaned, Mira even refused help from anyone when she took her leave to tidy up.

"Enjoy your time," Mira had told Vera earlier.

And oh, she *was*.

"Happy birthday to you, my Vera," Vaslav finished, keeping the same harmonized tone. She hadn't realized how good his gravelly voice sounded signing a song and made a mental note to get him to do that again later.

Despite the song being over, he kept them rocking in a slow semi-circle, some bastardization of a waltz. Wrapped in his arms with her face tucked—hiding, and smiling—against his throat, she didn't care if they danced properly or not. Every soft kiss he grazed upon her forehead during and after his serenade, cemented her right there with him.

Present.

Pleased.

"How does twenty-seven feel?" Vaslav asked her.

Vera laughed. "I don't know; you tell me. You've been here before. I'm still brand new."

Basically. That's what she planned to tell herself every year as she got older, anyway.

Even Vaslav chuckled at her joke while one of his hands stroked dangerously low on the small of her back.

Vera tipped her head back to see Vaslav's almost wistful gaze finding something to focus on at the far end of the room. It wasn't her mother who stood in the entry alcove between the dining room and a connected space meant for entertaining. Her father helped Igor to shove the leather sectional aside earlier. Doing so offered plenty of floorspace to dance.

Claire, busy showing off her pictures of the day to her husband, didn't seem to notice the other two people talking quietly, and very close. Only a few steps away in the corner, Igor and Hannah didn't notice the room, either, lost in their own conversation.

Staring at one another.

Vera couldn't help but pick up on it.

Nonetheless, whatever Vaslav found that interested him over her shoulder, it couldn't be important. In a blink, his attention came right back to where she wanted it.

On *her*.

"It's been a minute since I was that young, that's what I've settled on saying," he said.

Ah.

That's what had him looking lost in his eyes. She understood getting lost in another time of one's life. Even if that time hadn't necessarily been better.

He shrugged, too. Nonchalant.

The fading smile on his lips told her that he hadn't offered the entire truth. Or rather, he did, and simply phrased it differently than she might expect.

Complex people; complex thoughts.

"Are a lot of years like that for you?" she asked, choosing her words as carefully as he clearly had. "A lot of time?"

The edge of his mouth twitched like he almost answered without first thinking. Of course, he caught himself and only muttered, "If not fragmented, it's practically not there at all. Like white space and noise. I'm told that'll get worse."

She was ready for his next puzzle piece—the bit of information that helped to explain something else about this fascinating man. He only offered them occasionally, and she understood the reasons for that now. Part of him didn't always know what the real story was; the rest, he held terribly close.

She hadn't expected him to outright answer her with the truth, or rather—the reality he so easily handed to her with his words. That wasn't his typical way, and for a second, it took Vera off guard.

She didn't have a quick reply.

Vaslav was already moving on, saying, "Although,

what I know of it, it couldn't have been too bad of a year. My release was coming up."

Vera tried to imagine herself from thirteen to beyond her current age, under incarceration. *How did something like that change a person?* She couldn't quite wrap her head around it, or maybe the living, breathing man holding her was a testament to why she shouldn't.

Even though she shouldn't ask, Vera was too curious to stop herself. "What was that like—growing up in those places?"

Pulling in a deep breath and pausing to hold it before releasing the air in a long woosh, Vaslav's brow lifted in his contemplation. "How do you explain it if you don't know anything different?"

She had never thought of it like that, either.

Vaslav then untangled his left arm from hers to circle his fingers around her wrist before dragging their connected hands high enough for him to kiss her engagement ring, and the new matching band made of simple white gold resting beneath the larger diamond.

He picked the wedding band out. A classic choice, and she absolutely loved it. His, also one he chose, was a thicker band in the traditional gold. Amongst his many others, the wedding ring wasn't that amazing, and it certainly didn't stand out between ones topped with rubies and onyx stones.

Except she hadn't asked him to wear a wedding ring at all after they married, but he did so anyway. Without prompting, his band showed up wrapped in a similar box to hers from the same jeweler, according to the invoice. And now, she couldn't see any of his other rings except the one he chose to represent her.

"I can think of better times to have this particular conversation, no?" he asked before kissing her hand, and ring, again.

His gaze never left hers. They were still terribly close, too.

How was she to argue with that?

Vaslav arched an eyebrow, waiting for her reply.

Vera only whispered, "Fair enough."

On the room stereo, where Hannah had connected her phone via Bluetooth to play through a playlist of songs she created for the evening, the tune changed. Vaslav and Vera's semi- not-quite-a-waltz came to a stop. Too busy getting lost in the arms of her new husband—was that so bad?—and she hadn't noticed the lyrics of the singer sweeping through the space until her husband had stopped them on the spot. A song meant for a father and his daughter.

Although, no one else in the room except for them seemed to notice the change in tune first. Vera didn't step back from Vaslav right away, but his tight hold around her didn't loosen up, either.

"Did you pick the songs, or no?" he asked.

She grinned. "I didn't know Hannah even made the playlist until this morning, actually. I had very little to do with it."

Nothing about the wedding had been intricate in the details or planning. It might have seemed like it on the surface, but mostly, things fell together when she needed them to, and Vera was fine to let it happen. Maybe it wasn't a huge event—instead of the ballroom dance floor at a swanky hotel for her reception, she danced with her husband behind the safe walls of their home.

And that—*all of it*—was perfect.

She couldn't ask for more.

Vaslav smiled back. "Ah, well—she picked good songs."

Vera had to agree, and made a mental note to thank her friend in a special way once all of this was over, and she had the chance to do something meaningful for Hannah. The girl deserved it for simply coming through to do her part at the wedding when she hadn't even been asked to in the first place. Never mind the fact that Hannah's initial thoughts about the marriage had been less than great. What were best friends for?

"Oh—go, Demyan. I think this one's for you," Vera heard her mother urge.

As her father came closer, Vera noticed Igor slipping past Claire to leave the room. Hannah, and Vera's mother both had phones at the ready for what was to come.

Vaslav leaned in, and kissed Vera on the shell of her ear before murmuring, "Dance with your father and make the most of your time. I don't plan on letting you out of my sight for a few days after tonight. It's my time with you now, and we both know I've earned it."

His promise came laced with sin. The kind that set her nerves on fire, and had her mind racing with anticipation. By the gleam in his eye and smirk toying with his lips, Vaslav witnessed her inner war, and reveled in it.

"You shouldn't do that to me when we still have guests," Vera scolded under her breath, but it did nothing for the heat flooding her cheeks.

Vaslav winked as he pulled away, asking genuinely, "Do what?"

Vera shivered from his question; his dark words caressed her skin like the silk of her gown did with every movement she made. Despite picking a second, more appropriate dress to wear after the ceremony, she continued wearing the heavy gown. Tight to her body, it had been a risk. Silk always was a risky choice when without much structure underneath, the fabric could be unforgiving to parts of a woman's figure that she might prefer to hide. Soft and constricting at the same time, Vera couldn't stand the thought of taking it off.

Especially not after the way Vaslav had visually approved of her choice and wedding dress at the altar.

Demyan, too close for Vera to ignore now, cleared his throat. "Are we dancing?"

Vaslav held on to Vera's hand right down until only the tips of their fingers touched, before he finally let her go. "You are, comrade."

Cheeky prick.

He knew good and well what he was doing.

Vera would play along.

For now.

"Yeah, Papa," Vera said, turning with open arms ready for her father, "I think Hannah picked this one for us."

*

Hannah was sweet enough to add a second song to the playlist that was geared toward a father and daughter that gave Vera extra time to linger close to the safety of her father wrapped in his hug. Her forehead rested against Demyan's cheek while he regaled her with another of her childhood antics that

7

had them both in stitches. Her favorite in the bunch so far. That one, in particular, was how she'd decided that her younger brother, Roman—the only biological child between her parents—would be allowed to stay as a part of their family. After his birth, of course.

"He wanted to come for this," Demyan assured her.

For the fifth time. At least. He wasn't the first— even Claire said the same thing.

Demyan also pulled rank. Roman, most times unpredictable even when on his best behaviour, couldn't currently leave the country. He could, should his father want to take the risk of travelling his son with fake documents, but he opted not to.

She didn't blame him. Demyan was already on Interpol's watch list for more than a few reasons.

"I know," Vera replied. And she did.

Her father's sigh lasted just long enough to say he wasn't particularly happy about it, though. Some things never changed … or so she was told.

"I hope you know that I'm so happy you lived, Vera. That you got the chance when every card was stacked against you."

With his hand still tucked in hers, she used them both to poke playfully at his chest, earning her laugh. "You had a lot to do with that, too, Papa," she told him.

Lifting her head to see Demyan nod at her, she smiled wide.

"That, too, is true," he said. "I guess."

There was no guesswork to it. She lived, and he did everything he could to let her do it.

"I wouldn't be me without you, in a way. I wouldn't have been so willing to get out and live a life

I wanted had you not expected me to; had you not taught me to."

His eyes—Avdonin-blue as their family affectionately called it—the same as hers, softened. "I'll be honest," he said with a light chuff, "and say I did have a little hope that you might settle down closer to home. It would be easier to watch your family grow; I envisioned that, getting to do what my father did with me, but I know here is where you're meant to be."

That mattered more.

He didn't need to say it.

"To be fair," she said, trying to shrug the heavier emotions off her bare shoulders while also attempting not to burst her father's bubble further, "there are no plans for ... *growing*, as you said."

She didn't come right out and say she had no intentions of giving Demyan grandchildren. Her statement should have been clear enough.

"Oh well," was all he said.

Not oh-*pause*-well. No. Just *oh well*, no surprise at all, like it didn't even make a difference.

Their slow waltz never missed a beat. His smile didn't falter, either. Vera wouldn't admit that his unconcerned response helped to ease the anxiety about her choice. She was a woman, after all—maybe she wondered if there was something about motherhood that she would miss out on. It still wasn't quite enough to change her mind on the topic of kids, however. If the question needed a life-altering event to be answered, well that spoke for itself.

"How long are you and Ma planning to stay in Russia?" she asked, then, redirecting their topic of conversation to a better one. "And did they let you extend your stay in town?"

"They were happy to," Damian returned with a grin. "But I'm paying a small fortune weekly for that bed and breakfast—it's good money. No one smart would refuse, hmm?

It paid to be rich. So to speak.

"But how long are you staying?"

His ability to pay for lodging Claire liked in Dubna was only part of her initial question, and not even the most important one. Vera had a suspicion as to why her father opted to answer one rather than the other. Because he had some scheme going on currently with Vaslav. Evident by their many phone conversations lately that usually occurred in the late evenings. Which meant business.

Obviously, mafiya.

Demyan did nothing but stare at his daughter, proving her silent thoughts right, too. "At least a couple of weeks. I assume. There are always things that take time, Vera."

She didn't press for more information, and was lucky to get what she did, likely.

His scant details about the coming weeks—and her parents' last-minute plans to stay in the country longer than expected—would have to be dealt with later, or whenever Vera got the time seeing as how she couldn't forget Vaslav's earlier promise after their dance. It still lingered on the back of her mind.

Hannah popped in behind Demyan, and tapped him on the shoulder with a tinkling laugh when she caught him off guard. The song also changed at the same time. Like perhaps her friend had that little trick planned. Hannah's grin said she might. The song was one with a faster beat, too. Exactly the girls' style.

"I can cut in now, right?" Hannah asked.

Damian didn't even hesitate. "Of course."

"Are you going to let him do the work of taking off the dress?" Hannah looped their arms together, and flashed a cheeky grin.

Vera, already swinging her hips to the faster beat, admitted, "That might have unintentionally been the plan."

"Are you doing a honeymoon away from Moscow later?"

"Probably not, but I don't care."

She was happy.

Could Hannah see it?

Her friend glowed with her own inner joy. It was hard to miss. "Well, you know the villa is taken care of with me, right?"

Vera winked. "Oh, so you're not planning to throw one of your infamous parties, then?"

"Are you giving me permission?"

As quick as ever.

Hannah couldn't turn the opportunity down.

Vera barked a sharp laugh. "Hell no."

Hannah pouted her painted-red lips exaggeratedly. "You're no fun." She nodded at the sectional where it'd been shoved against the wall. "Let's sit."

Vera's feet throbbed.

A little.

She still didn't regret opting for the shoes with a small heel, but she didn't refuse Hannah's offer when it meant she could rest her feet, either.

With a sigh, she agreed, "Yeah I need a break. Nobody told me that somebody had created an entire playlist of music to dance to."

"You didn't need to worry about that, too."

Hannah beamed—the smug pride clear—as the two women fell into the plush leather cushions of the couch side by side. Her friend's eyes twinkled in that familiar way that Vera only associated with Hannah.

"And thank you for doing that," Vera said, wanting her friend to know just how much she appreciated every little touch Hannah put on her special day. The memories were absolutely everything to Vera. "The music, the breakfast with my mom this morning. Even—"

Hannah lifted one shoulder, interjecting with, "At this point, you're basically my only friend. And that's fine. I needed to get away from the noise everyone else makes to figure out who I am. Yeah, Vera, I'd do anything for you. You already kind of did that for me."

It was that moment when one of the men who had slipped out of the room earlier decided to make a return.

Igor nodded with a tight smile at Vera's mother and father as he passed them in the entryway. It softened with more kindness when his attention landed on Vera and Hannah. He came to stand in front of them, folding his hands behind his back. Beside her, Hannah instantly fidgeted; she glanced down but it didn't hide the new wash of color in her cheeks. Vera couldn't miss it.

Hell, Igor hadn't even opened his mouth to speak yet.

Yep.

Hannah had a crush.

Vera didn't know exactly when it started, or where. She didn't point out that the awkward panic Hannah had first felt around Igor was practically non-existent now.

"Do you want to have a dance with me, sweets?" Igor asked.

Hannah was quick to look up then, but not before tossing a glance at Vera. "Maybe, yeah."

"Is it maybe, or yeah?"

That question had Hannah smirking back, probably ready with a quippy reply.

Vera decided to leave the two to their verbal foreplay, and whatever else was happening. "I'm going to find my husband," she said, pushing up from the couch.

The two she left behind didn't say goodbye.

Or they didn't have the sense to.

2.

"You're back to that again, yeah?"

Vaslav didn't acknowledge the fact that he had heard Igor's question from the doorway of the den. Instead, he took another swig from the glass filled with ice and cold water. Only then did he spin around on his office chair to face the waiting man. Igor stayed in the doorway, haloed by the brighter hallway lights. He didn't move past the threshold. A new thing the man had started doing ever since Vaslav drew the invisible line he refused to cross between them.

The Kiril line.

"Say that again?" Vaslav asked, pretending like he hadn't heard Igor and inviting the man to stick his foot even farther into his mouth. "I didn't quite catch it, Igor."

He didn't actually wait for Igor to respond before he tossed back the handful of pills he'd been hiding in his palm. What liquid remained in his glass helped to wash the pills back.

Bogdan was all too happy to write a prescription if his patient promised to follow directions and show up to appointments—he even made it possible for Vaslav to have his medications delivered.

He didn't necessarily promise to follow *all* of the doctor's rules, even if he did say what he had to in order to make the man more agreeable. It was what it was.

Vaslav was *trying*.

What more did they all want?

"Does Vera know that you're back to popping pills and chugging liquor?" Igor asked, getting straight to the point the second time around. "Alone in your den in the dark, I might add."

Usually, Vaslav liked blunt and straightforward. Igor was lucky that at the moment, Vaslav at least *respected* the fact that he was both.

"I'm happy to see you've found your balls," he told his oldest friend.

"And that's not an answer to my question," Igor returned, still chill where he stood in the doorway with his hands tucked loosely in his pockets.

Vaslav gave Igor credit—if due, so be it.

The man showed up for the day. He even wore the pale yellow vest and bowtie set that Vera picked out to match Hannah's gown. Igor didn't complain, wasn't late, and never let his true mood be known to the rest of the people around them that day. He let the woman of the hour have her day to shine and be adored, and Vaslav truly appreciated that from Igor.

All things considered.

Setting the glass to the top of his desk, Vaslav pushed two fingers down through freezing ice cubes until the tips of his digits were able to touch the mouthful of liquid that remained at the very bottom. Pulling his fingers back out just as fast, he flicked the droplets of water that had gathered at the tips in Igor's direction. The other man didn't so much as flinch.

Vaslav snorted. "It's water and ice. Not vodka, or anything else, yeah? Mira brought it to me. She knows I need to take my pills around this—"

"Since when do you keep a schedule for your Vicodin and sleeping pills?"

"It was more than just those," Vaslav shot back hotly.

Not that it did him any favors to admit it.

Igor didn't react except to say, "But that's not really the point, is it?"

Dammit.

Instead of outright explaining the schedule of his current meds—and because he refused to feed Igor's current need to provoke Vaslav's aggression—he yanked open a drawer on the desk, and from it, pulled a pillbox made up of twenty-one steel boxes.

Three rows of seven.

Morning, noon, and night.

Each box had a top, engraved with the day of the week and designated time of day, that could be easily flipped open. At first glance, one might not see the engravings depending on the light. It didn't look like the standard pillbox that came to *his* mind. That's also what he liked the most about it.

Vaslav popped open the next evening's designated box and dumped out the few pills waiting inside to the top of his desk. They scattered across the old gloss until every single one came to a stop in different places. All the while, Igor didn't move a muscle.

Pointing at one house-shaped pill, Vaslav said, "That's the only one in the bunch that matters, no? Apparently, the studies show it slows the dementia's eventual progression when started early and taken long enough. But we're talking what they've known for maybe thirty, forty years, so—"

What real effect it might have on him was still yet to be determined, and by the time it really mattered, would he even know the difference?

Vaslav shrugged, letting his statement cut off abruptly because frankly, he wanted to move on. He nodded at another pill on the desk. White and circular. "A migraine med that probably *won't* help, but I had to indulge Bogdan to get the things I really wanted." He pointed at a pale pink cylinder pill that had tumbled farther than the rest to the middle of the desk. "A sedative for the evening. Swears it'll knock out a horse. At my worst, it makes me feel like a spineless slug."

He didn't bother with the rest of the pills. They were only meant to manage the worst symptoms that came from the other medications, or the mood stabilizer he took every morning that helped only slightly with his more neurotic behaviors and thoughts, but what difference did it make?

Vaslav scooped the pills up into his palm and dropped them back into their respective box. "The pillbox was a wedding gift from my wife— unironically, I want to enjoy these years with her. More than me, *she* deserves that, too. So yes," Vaslav said, shrugging and he snapped the top closed. "She does know. *Spasibo*."

Igor cleared his throat and shifted from foot to

foot. The frank honesty made him uncomfortable, as it should. That was the point.

"Good to know you've been keeping up on all of that, then," Igor finally settled on saying.

A good minute after the fact.

Vaslav didn't feel a need to point out that his friend's busy schedule—and his recent displeasure—kept him more distant than usual. Both were valid excuses. Vaslav blamed his friend for neither. Mere months ago, it would have been unheard of for Igor to miss out on Vaslav's day-to-day activities.

"Demyan mentioned your plans for a dinner," Vaslav hedged, opting to take their conversation in a new direction. "One where you would like my wife to make an appearance."

Igor shrugged in the halo of light spilling in where he'd inched slightly closer to straddling the doorway's threshold. This far at the end of the house, the music from the party was barely a murmur. "I think her presence, and rings, cement what it all means. I like to think it gives credence to the marriage and retirement rumors."

"There are no rumors about my *retirement*."

A sigh answered that indignant remark.

"Yet," Igor replied.

Well …

"I'm just not fond of the word," Vaslav said. Such a thing didn't exist in the true sense. Thieves had reversed their spiders for decades before him to say it was so, but he wasn't foolish enough to believe that would be enough to protect him.

At least, not forever.

It was what it was.

Igor wanted an easy transition in the brotherhood

as he took over. Vaslav, of course, pointed out that in the midst of reorganizing power and communication structures amongst thieves was always easier said than done. Igor's efforts would be in vain—the wings waited with someone to strike when big changes happened in the criminal world.

Either way, it was a lesson better learned. Things like that couldn't be taught, and Vaslav had to take a step back in that regard. He no longer had a desire to be the man constantly looking over his shoulder. Props to Igor for taking up the job—whether he wanted to or not.

"She can't be used as a prop," Vaslav warned.

Vera wouldn't turn into someone's next target, and certainly not because of someone else's—mainly Igor—stupidity,

"At most," Igor said, "she'll be a passing moment in a significant day."

Vaslav chuckled dryly. "Listen to you— romanticizing it."

"Oh, don't worry, Vas," Igor replied as he turned away to leave, "I know good and well how lonely it is at the top. Also, compliments of *you*."

Before the man could totally disappear beyond the doors, Vaslav called at Igor's back, "What's the latest news on Kiril?"

As he knew the question would—it stopped Igor's leave in his tracks. "You don't care."

"Not what I asked, either."

Igor's shoulders lifted with a heavy exhale. "Looks like he'll be out doing his thing again next week. Or around then. I may have paid for a decent legal representative to make a few visits."

"And a few calls for him, too, I imagine."

Igor didn't confirm it, but Vaslav didn't need him to.

Vaslav himself might not have been willing to step in on the boy's behalf, but Igor had every right to the moment he agreed to take over for his former boss. Vaslav's word was only law until it wasn't, after all.

Igor glanced over his shoulder, finding Vaslav still sitting alone in the darkness of his den. "I'll have to keep my eye on him, of course."

Right …

Because Kiril's upcoming freedom meant very little at the end of the day. It certainly wasn't a guarantee that trouble wouldn't follow the kid—or his connection to the mafiya—beyond the bars of a cell. It also didn't promise that he hadn't talked.

"Good luck with that," Vaslav muttered.

Igor shook his head, replying in kind, "Yeah." Then, he asked, "Aren't you getting back to the party?"

"Is it—a party?"

"You know what I mean."

Vaslav scrubbed a hand down his jaw. "I need a break from the noise." And hell, maybe his wife would come looking for him, and then he could get an early start on the better portion of his evening. Wouldn't that be grand? "Why don't you go dance with that green-eyed woman? You two certainly looked like you might enjoy it."

"Smooth, Vas," Igor bitched under his breath as he exited the office. "Really smooth."

"Being lonely," Vaslav called back, "doesn't also mean your bed needs to be cold, old friend."

Another lesson the man would be wise to learn from Vaslav.

*

Vera had stepped inside Vaslav's office only a few short minutes after Igor left, and the second she closed and locked the door behind her—assured he wasn't hiding in the dark with a severe migraine—it was on.

All Vaslav needed to get hard was Vera alone in a room with him. Fuck the door, it didn't even have to be locked. Although, she was getting better at remembering to do so. Of course, once she had heard the laughter and music rising from down the hall, his plans turned dirty.

Why not?

No one would miss her for fifteen minutes.

Surely.

And even if they did—oh, well.

Vera was *all his* now. She agreed the second she let him slip a wedding band down her finger. Who was he to ignore the constant hunger that churned in his gut for the woman whenever she was within his reaching distance?

Vera taught Vaslav an important thing about people that he hadn't given much attention to before. Love's language. Different for everyone, the way they showed their love was often what they also needed to receive. Hers was tangled in a deep web of emotions and desires. Wrapped up entirely in her long conversations and ever-present empathy. Soft-hearted, but only sometimes soft-spoken.

His love language wasn't exactly the same. Often not kind or sweet—his needs were usually selfish, and self-serving. But *pleasing*. He craved her. All of her. At every second of any given day of the week. She was always on his mind, and so were the things he wanted to be doing with her. Whether that was bending her over the closest flat surface, or watching her read for an hour while she laid in his lap. Whatever it was, he wanted it—she was his; she said so—and he greedily took all of it from her.

But ...

There was always a but.

Vaslav could be unhealthily obsessed with the time he consumed of Vera's attention. As she, and people she loved, kindly pointed out to him. Her mother had done it while his mouth was full of food she made that he thought was to die for. Vera, on the other hand, had delivered the news in her own special way. While her smeared lipstick still stained the base of his cock.

He was trying to be better about it all.

Just not tonight.

It was his wedding night, too, after all.

Vaslav figured that counted for something, even if that, too, was selfish. So be it.

The very second Vera had crossed the room, clearly knowing his plans and not finding a problem, she sealed her fate. She'd tumbled, laughing breathlessly, into his lap. She was always as needy and greedy for sex as him, and frankly, he loved it.

Loved *her*.

"We've got maybe fifteen minutes before somebody comes looking for us," he'd mumbled against their first messy kiss.

Fifteen minutes was just enough.

Vera had no shame about turning her back to him in his lap. Straddled over either side of the chair with her feet high on the armrests, she didn't say a thing about her beautiful gown or how he might ruin and wrinkle the silk when he yanked the heavy skirt up around her waist. No, she just wanted to be touched. Rocking wantonly into every graze of his wandering hands, moaning when he rubbed her how she liked overtop her panties while he kissed up the side of her neck. She was all too willing to help them both by lifting up for him to do his business.

With her bent over in front of him, he could see she was already wet right through the cotton gusset of her white lace panties. It only took a little maneuvering on his part to get his pants unzipped and shuffled down enough to get his cock free.

Already hard and aching.

She shimmied her ass against him when he pulled her white lace panties to the side, and yanked her hips back down, sitting her onto his cock. He speared into her slick heat that enveloped him in the heaven between her thighs. She wiggled, full of him. The gasp she made when she seated down on him was a sound he'd like to replay on repeat.

"*Good Christ*," he uttered against her trembling shoulder, praying and praising at the same time. Why was it *always* so good? He'd fucked her that morning, too. Before her friend showed up just beyond an ungodly hour with promises of a special breakfast. Vera had emptied him, then, too, but it wasn't enough. He wanted it all again. As soon as they were done—he could already taste her tartness and feel how warm she'd be when she came dripping on his lap like this.

It had a way of making her rain. Something about the angle she liked. It was a good thing the den connected to the rooms upstairs so he could at least change fast.

Vera hissed when he shifted her up and down on his lap, grinding his dick harder and deeper inside of her. But she didn't shy away from the overfilled sensation he knew it caused her. Instead, she shoved back into him, a silent demand for more.

"You love it when I do that—don't you?" he asked, taking a taste of her skin between each and every word. "When I take you first, nothing else," he groaned when she initiated the next push and pull between their connected hips. All it took was the flex of her inner muscles to make him fucking weak. "My greedy girl—you like it when it's my cock that opens you up."

Vera's laugh was light, high, and sweet when she breathed back, "It only stings a little."

Yes.

And she liked that, too.

So wet that every stroke of his cock into her cunt brought with it slippery sounds, one of her hands fell between her thighs. Her fingertips stroked between their sensitive, meeting bodies. Teasing him when she lifted to stroke his cock, slick with her juices as he pulled out of her, and then sighing when those same fingertips toyed with her clit when he slammed back into her.

He might have ripped the thin netting of her white stockings when she rocked harder onto him, but she didn't appear to mind.

"Hurry up—put those fingers of yours to use," he told her. "You better come before someone knocks while you're fucking squealing."

Her fingernails dug into his left thigh where she

had previously found stability. Sharp and pinching, it only earned her a chuckle. "I do *not* squeal."

At that, he outright laughed.

"You just had to go and turn it into a challenge, *kisska*, yeah? You still have to tell them all goodbye. Should have thought of that."

3.

"How is your honeymoon so far?" Claire asked, the very first question she had after greeting Vera when she picked up her mother's call.

Claire couldn't see the way Vera's face flushed with heat, and she was grateful for that. There was only one way to describe the past few days as a newly married woman to a very particular husband: *insatiable*.

"Well?" Claire pressed at Vera's silence.

"Where's Papa?" Vera returned, cheeky on purpose.

Claire laughed. "Never mind, then. That tells me more than enough. Someone's keeping you busy."

What else needed said?

"Yep," Vera replied, happily.

"As Vaslav should," she thought her mother said back.

Vera couldn't be sure of Claire's final words for their conversation because the crackle of static over the speaker as it was passed over to someone new cut out the last bit of the reply.

Her father spoke next.

"I wasn't quite far enough away not to hear that, anyway," he mumbled as Vera cackled.

"I thought you were sleeping—*really*," Claire insisted in the background.

"Trying to," Demyan grumbled. "Someone loves to make phone calls first thing in the morning. In bed with her husband, too."

As Claire had been the one to call her, Vera didn't pay much attention to the early morning hour until her father mentioned it. As a child, she could remember his motto about not rolling his ass out of bed before nine, if he could help it.

Life, kids, and duty often got in the way.

Then, she had another thought.

"Shouldn't you be up already?" she asked her father. "Don't you have lunch in the city this afternoon?"

Silence answered her question about a lunch he might not have known she had any clue about. A lunch she only had the details for because Vaslav had also intended on attending until the low-grade migraine he'd been suffering on and off with for a couple of days finally came to it's unbearable peak. Not even the medication meant to sedate him had helped the night before.

He wasn't in any state to go *anywhere*. Even if the worst of it had finally waned, leaving the two of them soaking in the jacuzzi tub in the very wee hours of the morning where he explained about the lunch he was supposed to attend the next day.

Igor would also be in attendance. No other women were to join the men, however. A purposeful move on his and Igor's part as the restaurant they'd be dining in was owned by a man with significant ranking in the organization. Demyan would be seen with the current boss, and Igor, before any official announcement or event could happen. The reason for all of these careful plans and public meetings?

Vaslav's retirement.

She didn't have the first clue why all the pomp and circumstance was needed, but those were the kinds of details Vaslav hadn't seemed interested in discussing.

Nonetheless, he wouldn't be attending the meeting when he was barely able to lift his head from a pillow at the moment. She made the call to Igor whom she assumed would pass the news and change of plans onto Demyan.

According to Vaslav, it didn't matter.

Without him, the lunch still served its purpose. Apparently, all it took for Vas to share *his* criminal dealings was a marriage bed. Vera liked to think a little trust and love worked to her favor there, too.

Not that Vaslav would say as much.

"I guess I better get my ass moving for that," her father said after letting the silence extend on long enough that she had wondered if he fell back asleep.

"It is a two-hour drive," Vera replied. "And we both know Vaslav doesn't like when people are late."

Even if he wouldn't be there—that didn't make a difference to Vaslav.

Demyan answered back with a scoff mixed into a laugh.

"Will you at least admit you like him a little?" Vera asked while her father's grumblings about difficult—and fucking crazy—men continued.

In the background, much to Demyan's annoyed

sigh that rattled through the speakers of the phone, Claire said clearly, "Oh, don't worry. He does."

*

Not more than five minutes after Vera ended the phone call with her parents, Mira joined her in the set of suites across from the master rooms. Empty but for a pile of dusty cardboard boxes piled high in the corner, the bedroom suites featured a similar layout as the master with a main sitting room—larger than the spaces it connected to—leading to a bedroom with an en suite bath, and other rooms with similarly dark, bare hardwood floors.

"It needs a good wax," Mira told her when she walked into the main room to find Vera bent over inspecting the condition of the floors.

Vera popped up straight, and turned with a smile. "Are all the floors original?"

"Most," the older woman replied. "These ones are."

Taking the cup of tea Mira offered on a tea plate, Vera nodded. "I see, thank you."

"The contractor called," Mira said while Vera lifted the cup for a sip of nutty tea. The news perked her interest, and Mira didn't miss it, laughing before she clarified, "He called to say he was at the gate right before I brought your tea up. By the time he walks the icy drive, I've still got plenty to make it down and greet him before he can ring the bell."

Vera rolled her eyes. "I can't believe he makes the man walk from the gate."

"Most everyone does. Even the mail. Mr. Pashkov's rule."

Right.

And there were a few of those.

Mira shrugged, then, her grin turning conspiratorial when she explained, "But I've heard the Christmas cards for those people come with generous gifts for anyone who is required to visit the property. And nobody's complained."

Vera's brow lifted in reply.

The older woman winked, then. "Mr. Pashkov's unspoken and often private generosity has treated the town and people gratefully."

"And they reply in kind."

Mira passed a playful shrug as she turned to survey the bare walls all around them. "You said it, not me. I heard you had plans for a couple of things?"

"The big windows," Vera replied, widening her hands to frame the large, tall rectangular windows facing every four corner of the outer rooms except the dark sitting room in the middle. "I'd like to knock out a couple of walls and give it a bit of air exchange. That'll help to keep the moisture from all the plants at a bearable level. It won't rot the walls, anyway."

"It does get a lot more sun throughout the day on this side of the house," Mira agreed. "It's a good spot for a plant room."

It might be good for Vaslav, too, but Vera didn't say as much out loud. He obviously enjoyed nature, and her penchant to bring as much of it as she could inside certainly couldn't do him any harm.

Only time would tell.

"Did I also hear there might be a studio upstairs?" Mira asked.

Vera waved a finger in the other woman's direction, only a little bit amused that Mira could manage to hear private conversations—and politely let Vera know as such after. "That was *Vaslav's* idea," she pointed out. "Besides, I don't think I really want to do that. I don't need my own private studio to dance in."

Mira's sober tone matched the heaviness in Vera's chest when she said, "It's okay if you do, though. And even better, if you can."

Shoving her hands into the back pockets of her high-waisted skinny jeans, Vera replied, "Yeah, I guess."

Mira didn't press the topic. "Vaslav won't be heading to the city for lunch, I suppose?"

One of the things Vaslav admitted to his new bride that he looked forward to the most once she moved in with him was that he wouldn't need to depend so much on Mira. In fact, he wanted practically no one within breathing distance of him when his migraines made him sick, mean, and angry. Mira couldn't really subdue her desire to help, but with Vera there, she didn't have to feel so guilty about taking a step back.

"No, he probably won't leave his bed today," Vera settled on saying.

They could figure out tomorrow when it came.

Mira nodded at the news like it wasn't surprising, but the glance she shot over her shoulder, her line of vision taking her attention beyond the door and across the hall to the master's doors, gave her silent thoughts away.

That, or Vera had simply become more perceptive of those things in the time that Vaslav entered her life. His close scrutiny of people was not lost on her.

"Was there something Vaslav needed to know?" Vera asked.

Mira's gaze quickly snapped back to Vera. Her initial hesitance made any rebuttal she might try weak before she could get the words out. "I—"

"Would he care if you didn't tell him?"

That made Mira pause for even longer. "Actually," she replied after more than a handful of seconds had passed, "he wouldn't. He's fine with where she's found herself and how it will inevitably end. It can wait. God knows they've probably already been paid to see her through the end, if need be."

It was the unidentified *she* that Mira mentioned which caused Vera to blurt out, "Well, I could always tell him."

Who was this *she*? And why exactly did Mira talk about her predicament—whatever it was—like Vera should already know about it?

As it was, Vera did have a jealous streak. No, that wasn't true. Possessive was more like it. Protective of her husband, too; that certainly fit the bill.

"Later," Vera assured Mira, trying not to feel too guilty about her white lie. "I'll tell him later if he's in a better mood."

Mira didn't catch the lie. "Not even a better mood makes news about his mother easier to swallow. The hospital called with an update. Not that it was anything good."

Oh.

Vera tried not to show her surprise that the cause of her irritation wasn't exactly unknown. In a way. The few passing comments Vaslav made about his mother let her know the important things. They weren't close, he didn't care to be, and Vera should count herself lucky that she hadn't met the woman personally.

"I didn't realize she was so … sick," Vera said, choosing her words carefully.

Mira showed little sympathy. "Natalia spiraled quite badly these past few weeks. Eventually, every party ends."

Given her age, Vera thought the woman might have said goodbye to the party decades ago.

"Either way," Mira muttered in a sigh as she turned to face the bare, brown walls again, "she's better where she is. And as Vaslav told me when the doctor first called, even that is more than she deserves."

That statement should have ended whatever curiosity that remained in Vera about Vaslav's mother. If even Mira, a woman who showed unwavering kindness, could say a woman deserved her agony without even her son knowing she was going through it, then who was Vera to argue with it?

Too bad curiosity didn't work like that, though.

*

"H-hello?" Hannah's groggy voice answered. After Vera's second call. It almost went to voicemail like the first.

"Are you still sleeping?" Vera asked.

Crawling close to two in the afternoon, even that was a little long for Hannah to be sleeping in. Had that been Hannah in Vera's shoes, she would have questioned it, too.

Hannah's responding groan was only mildly annoyed. "I can hear you judging me, Vera."

"Bullshit." But it was midday, *mid-week*, and that truly said something. Hannah didn't particularly have a lot to do in Moscow at the moment, but she also had practically no responsibilities. Vera couldn't help but think her friend might be taking advantage of both those things. As she should. "Were you out last night?"

Hannah's muffled laugh crackled through the speakers. "Who's nosy now?"

"Shut up."

They were both terrible.

It was what it was.

Hannah sighed, then, admitting, "I did go out—he was here when I got back. Stayed later than he promised this time, too."

Vera's eyebrows shot high. There was only one possible *he* that she knew about in Hannah's life at the moment. "Who—Igor?"

Another groan was Hannah's only reply.

That wasn't enough for Vera.

"Are you serious?" she asked her friend in a rush despite trying to tamper her tone.

While she'd closed the connected doorway to the stairwell that led up to their private rooms, the man could sometimes hear a water drop falling from a tap at the other side of the house when the sharp sensitivity came in to torture his pain a little more.

"And you didn't call to tell me—wait," Vera said, stopping mid-sentence when she realized the more important thing Hannah had said. "*This time*? When did it happen the first time?"

"You're too loud when I've just woken up."

"It's practically two!"

Hannah hemmed and hawed a while longer before muttering, "The night of your wedding, okay?"

Right.

Vera could have guessed.

So it brought her right back to the first thing she'd asked Hannah which was now more like a joking accusation. "And you didn't even call me."

Hannah's soft, tired laugh told her friend they both knew that neither was all that mad. "It hasn't even been a full week since you got married. I was trying to let you have time with your husband."

Fair enough.

"But I also need time with you," Vera said. "We should do that. Soon."

That perked Hannah's interest.

"How soon?"

"What are you doing this weekend?"

"Not much," Hannah deadpanned, but she didn't offer anything more to explain the change in her tone. Vera opted not to push.

She also chose not to mention the paperwork for a recent wire transfer that had been paid to a facility in the city that she found on Vaslav's desk while chatting with her friend. He had a bad habit of letting private documents lay around where it could easily be found if someone was looking. Or more concerningly, it was a sign that Vaslav was having trouble remembering certain short-term memory things.

Vera would put the transfer invoice away, but she wouldn't deny that she had also been looking for something like it when she stumbled on it, too. The call with her friend had simply been a justifiable excuse to wander mostly alone. If he found out, and asked.

It wasn't a hospital, like Mira had said. Not according to the invoice. The facility currently housing Vaslav's ill mother dealt more in psychiatrics.

In fact, it's name was Roseville Facility of Psychiatrics. While Vera had not called the number for the facility yet, she planned to.

"The better question," Hannah said, drawing Vera back into the conversation, "what are *you* doing this weekend?"

"Pretty sure I'm coming to visit you."

"Yay," her friend crowed. "But remember, whatever we do, we have to bring your mom, too."

Yeah.

Couldn't forget that, either.

4.

The roads leading out of Dubna were more familiar than ever to Vera now. It was too early in the drive to be lost in her thoughts while the vehicle passed the long stretches of snow-covered trees and fields, but that's exactly where she found herself.

Her driver—Igor lately, when possible and only if she really needed it because he, too, was busy—made her contemplative silence easier by focusing on the road ahead instead of attempting to engage his quiet passenger.

Her thoughts weren't such a bad place to be at the moment. At least there, she could remember Vaslav's tired smile and chuckle that morning when she told him her plans to spend Friday and Saturday with her mother and Hannah in the city. She hadn't expected him to refuse her—and he didn't—considering Demyan and Claire would travel home within a week or so.

"Get your time in with them," he had told her, his

voice still gruff with exhaustion. With his nose and mouth nuzzling her neck while he delivered those words, Vera was nearly willing to call her weekend plans off entirely.

Almost.

Vaslav, smartly, gave her a reason not to when he had added, "I need some sleep. I'll be here."

Rest—when he felt reasonably well—was impossible for Vaslav when Vera was near. A part of her adored it as much as she hated it only because exhaustion made everything worse for Vas. Oh, she couldn't, and wouldn't, complain that he wanted to spend every good day he had wrapped up in her, filling his every moment however he pleased because it pleased her, too.

But he paid for it, too.

She saw it as clear as day.

It didn't matter how tired he was from days of a constant, unforgiving migraine that kept him awake, nothing would close his eyes if she was the thing standing in front of him. Almost like he was scared to miss something. Or maybe, like he was trying to soak up every second of them and their time together that he could. Did he imprint it all to his mind like she did to hers?

Better yet—would Vas keep his memories of them like she would always do? That wasn't such an easy answer, but frankly, so few things about them *were* easy.

And I also never asked for that, Vera told herself in the back of the quiet car. She truly didn't believe that easy love would feel the way hers did. It took effort—and yes, certainty—to choose to love a person, a man, like Vaslav Pashkov.

A man who rarely apologized even when he was wrong; the same person who kissed softly, killed quickly. He didn't even try to teeter on the line between good and bad. The man knew which side he stood on, and had no issue with it. Unforgiving, unrepentant, and he needed to be loved in much the same way.

Or that's what she told herself, anyhow.

"How do Americans say it," Igor mused from the driver's seat of the Mercedes SUV, although he didn't pose it as a question. The first words he had spoken to her that day other than a polite hello and the confirmation that he could drive her to Noble Row. His sudden desire to chat made Vera pay attention.

Even if she was very confused.

"What?" she asked.

"The saying," the man returned.

Vera was still drawing a blank. "I need more to go on."

"The thoughts one, no?" Igor glanced into the rearview mirror to get Vera in his sights as he quirked his right eyebrow and added, "And the coin."

Oh.

Finally, it clicked for Vera. Laughing a little, and earning a chuffed laugh from Igor, she asked, "Do you mean—*a penny for your thoughts*?"

Igor nodded, but his attention had already returned to the road ahead. "Yes, that one."

"Is that even American?"

"Who'd know—that wasn't the point."

Right. Because he'd been asking—a penny for *her* thoughts.

"What changed?" Vera asked, and at the prompt of his questioning glance he tossed over his shoulder, she added, "No offense, but it's not like you've been very talkative."

Igor didn't deny it. "Things often weigh on my mind, yes? It's my personal deal with the devil, or so I was told."

"Oh," she exclaimed, honestly surprised. "I thought maybe you were mad at me, too."

"Who else am I mad at?"

Vera had better things to do than play word games on a long—and relatively boring—drive, so she went straight for the gut when she said, "Are you telling me that you're *not* mad at Vaslav, then?"

Igor remained silent.

She had her answer.

"But," the man manning the vehicle said, speaking up first, "that doesn't also mean I am mad at you."

Vera didn't understand that at all. Why wouldn't he be angry with her? She didn't need Igor to say he cared for and looked after young Kiril for her to have already put those details together. And if not for what Vaslav had planned regarding the ownership of The Swan House, and planting a forged deed in the office of a dead man during an active investigation into said malfeasance, then Kiril wouldn't have found himself in trouble.

She wasn't dumb.

Vera connected the fucking dots.

"You thought I blamed you?" Igor asked when Vera's silence in the front seat stretched on.

She shrugged as if it would help her explain, but the meek action didn't even catch the man's attention in the front seat. "I've been told I do that sometimes—take on faults that are not my own."

Old habits were hard to break.

Igor's tired sigh echoed from the front seat, and he visibly tightened his knuckles around the steering wheel until the leather squeaked. "For what it's worth," he told her, "very little about what has happened can be drawn back to you. And it doesn't matter anyway. Kiril is fine."

That was news to her.

"Define *fine*."

She didn't miss the roll of his eyes, but he answered nonetheless. "I took care of it."

Of him. She heard what he didn't say.

"Just because Vaslav refused to do something didn't also mean I had to," Igor said in a low mutter. "Mind you, don't expect to see the kid hanging around like he used to. I've got plans for Kiril. Not one of them includes him going back to jail."

"And you think he will," Vera pressed. "Get himself in more trouble, I mean. If he's around—"

Us, she almost said.

Igor interrupted before she could. "Things that are meant to happen *will* happen, Vera. That's not really my point, yeah?"

"So, what is?"

"Vas," the man said simply. "And Kiril, if I'm being fair. The kid's never going to tell Vas no. It doesn't even matter what he asked Kiril to do. The answer would unequivocally be *yes*."

Vera connected with that statement better than Igor could possibly understand. Actually, maybe Igor was the only other soul on the earth that could relate to what it was like to be unable to refuse Vaslav, Each just had a different reason for why.

"Right now, Kiril can't afford what saying yes might mean," Igor said after a moment.

41

The rain the weatherman had predicted would follow Moscow for the better part of the weekend chose that very moment to start dumping down. She felt the car slowing down as the heavy splatters soaked the passenger window and rolled across the glass in rivulets. Despite the wild way Igor tended to drive, even he wasn't willing to take the slushy, rural roads without a bit of extra caution in bad weather.

"But fuck," the man in front swore, pulling Vera from her otherwise wandering thoughts, "the thing is, I don't know why I even bother to try. Kiril would run his ass back to Dubna the second he could if Vas would have him." He slapped his hands to the steering wheel. "Like I said—what's gonna happen will happen."

She heard life was more fun when people let it all happen that way, but now didn't seem like the right time to point it out.

Igor settled back into silent driving while Vera opted to study the back of his bald head and tattooed neck. Barely visible, as only the beginnings of the red scratches could be seen over the rolled collar of his brown tweed jacket, she might not have asked about or noticed the claw marks had she not also been aware of Igor's private business. Specifically, with Hannah.

"You're not going to fuck my friend around, are you?" she asked Igor before losing her nerve. It had to be said, though.

Igor should *know*—somebody was looking out for Hannah. The girl had been through more than enough and deserved some happiness. Vera wasn't picky about where her friend found said happiness as long as it didn't eventually bring regret and pain.

Men were good at doing both.

Igor's head tipped to the side, and he let out an awkward laugh when in the rearview mirror, he watched her pointed stare travel from his gaze to the marks on the back of his neck. She thought that was clear enough.

His amusement drifted away when she remained stoic in response. Eventually, his focus went back to the road, and he asked her, "Why don't you worry about minding your own business, hmm?"

She had bad news for him.

"Hannah is my business."

It would do Igor well to learn that fact, and *fast*. Not even the sting of his stare finding her in the mirror once more scared her. Maybe it would have if she were a weaker woman, but hell ... if even the beast didn't scare her in the dark, then the king he promised to crown in his place certainly wouldn't, either.

"Got it?" Vera asked.

*

"I swear to God," Hannah said where she stood waiting behind Vera as her friend inspected the browning ends of a climbing vine plant. "I swear, Vera, I watered it just the way you said to. No more, no less. Five milliliters of blue food on Sundays. And I didn't touch that one, or any of them, when they were watered. Just like you said."

Touching wet plants was a great way to spread disease between different species, so it was one of the top rules Vera had written down for Hannah.

She smiled, not for one second doubting her friend.

The climbing vine that had grabbed onto the exposed red brick focus wall in the sitting room of the villa had already covered a significant portion of the right side from bottom to top. With only a little bit of directional help from Vera where she had started the plant in a moderately-sized pot on a nearby stool. The vine would continue to climb over the brick across to the window where it sought the little light it needed to thrive.

As long as they put it in a bigger pot.

Vera straightened to her full height, and shrugged off the worry she'd first felt when Hannah had mentioned a dying plant after she arrived. "It just needs repotted. Basically, it's as big as it's going to grow unless we give the roots more room. The nice thing about these is that they're hard to kill—they don't even get rootbound, really. But you can see some browning like that at the ends if their potential gets stunted."

Hannah nodded, surveying the brick section of wall again with new eyes. "Yeah, okay. I see what you're doing."

She winked. "Well, what you're doing now."

Vera earned herself a roll of Hannah's pretty twinkling eyes for that comment. "Right," her friend muttered. "Let's be honest—we're both surprised I haven't already killed a damn plant."

Well ...

Vera cackled out a laugh. "I still have faith in you."

Hannah's head bobbed dramatically in agreement, her frizzy curls bouncing wildly all the while. "Yes— *still.* Because who knows what's gonna happen."

She waved off Hannah's sarcastic self-deprecation, and tossed the messenger bag that had been weighing down her shoulder onto the nearby suede loveseat. Next went her purse. Like her shoes, she hadn't even bothered to drop her bags at the door like she usually would in her own home. The plants were serious business, but ...

"I'm not really that worried about you killing my plants," Vera said, her thick parka breaking her fall into the recliner by the window. "You're too Type-A. I knew it was fine once I made you a list of everything that needed what and how. You won't hurt something seriously enough that it can't be fixed."

Hannah crossed her arms over her chest, hiding the block words that spelled out a sports logo on the front of her hoodie, and cocked an eyebrow. "Vera, that list was thirty pages long and detailed the plants by *room*."

Vera grinned. "Yeah. And?"

"And?" Hannah asked back, scoffing. "And you say I'm the Type-A personality here."

Actually ...

"I never denied that I was also Type-A," Vera said, shrugging, "but I don't see the problem. Did you deviate from the stuff I put in the list?"

Hannah stuck out her tongue, and Vera answered the gesture in kind. Birds of a feather truly did flock together.

Before long, Vera had kicked off her shoes to the light-colored hardwood floors below while Hannah made a seat of her own on the nearby couch. She flicked the flatscreen off pause to resume the medical drama before replacing the remote on the coffee table where she'd also tossed Vera's bags.

"So," Hannah started, not looking away from the television, "who's the babysitter for the weekend?"

Vera's lengthy pause was made more awkward when Hannah turned to glance her way, clearly noticing. Her friend's brow jumped higher in a silent question.

"Oh, you thought I forgot about my annoying little roommate who's been missing for weeks?" Hannah asked as seriously as could be.

"Not really," Vera hedged.

Hannah flopped back on the arm of the couch with a sigh. "Igor told me the shite got arrested, anyway. Doesn't matter. *Somebody's* watching you," her friend pointed out, oh, so sure. "So, who is it?"

Not all that interested in the medical drama on the TV, Vera indulged Hannah's prodding. "I don't really know," she answered truthfully.

What would it hurt?

"How do you not kn—"

"I'm heading right back to Dubna tomorrow night, and we're not doing very much today," Vera clarified quickly. "It's not like I really needed someone. Besides, my mother and father have a guy on call from Igor's side of things if they need somebody, so he's sure to be there tomorrow when we take Ma to the spa."

Hannah didn't even try to hide the playful scowl she leveled on Vera at the news. Nothing could ruin her day like a babysitter. For good reason, sure. By now, Vera bet Hannah was entirely over being constantly watched by bodyguards and needing to always consider security. Not everyone wanted to live that life. Even if the bodyguards weren't for her now.

"It's hard to believe Vaslav let you out of the house without a friend to tag along, that's all," Hannah said.

"He's got other things on his mind," Vera replied

even if it was a lousy lie. Really, with her parents in the country and shifts in power happening amongst men at the top of Russia's criminal underground, Vera didn't care to ask if someone was watching her or who it would be. She simply assumed the choice had already been made, and taken care of—if it meant she was safe, and could return to Vas tomorrow night in one piece, then she didn't mind. The illusion of privacy was a sacrifice she would make.

Her father would love to see her swallowing that slice of humble pie.

"Where I am for a night and day is a minor detail," Vera added after a moment.

"Well," Hannah drawled, like she didn't believe what Vera said, "whoever the babysitter is, they won't be allowed in *Lele's*. No men in the spa. Just naked ladies. You know I was lucky to get us those spots last-minute, right?"

"But you did."

Hannah grinned. "I have my ways."

More like she had good connections, and Vera had the cash to make it worth the elite spa's while. Claire would love it, too. They needed the treat.

"Our appointment time is closer to the afternoon, right?" Vera asked.

"Yeah, like you said. Why?"

Hannah peeked over her shoulder at Vera who only shrugged in response.

"I might get up early tomorrow and take a run. It's been a while since I jogged Noble Row." The white lie slipped easily past Vera's lips, but she tried not to feel too guilty about it. For one, because Hannah didn't need to get dragged into Vera's dangerous— maybe—curiosities. Secondly, because she wanted the chance to make a phone call in total privacy. Some things, she just couldn't share with her friend.

"That's fine, you do that," Hannah said, not hiding the disdain in her words at all. "I don't run. Especially not in the snow."

5.

Drumming his fingers to the desk, and keeping his focus on the half-assed sketch of the property, Vaslav didn't have to watch the clock too much. Nothing made time move slower than a pair of eyes nailed to the face of a clock. Not that knowing as much made a huge difference to his urge to look.

It wasn't even like he had nothing else to do. The sketch of the property—with areas of interest marked out for a contractor in the spring—was a good example of better things he could be doing instead of time-watching. Even the tray of lunch Mira had brought into him over an hour earlier remained untouched on the side of his desk.

Frankly, his disinterest in the sandwich and rich red soup, no longer steaming hot like it had been at first, couldn't be connected to his distraction. That nonsense went straight back to his new cocktail of medications, and he wasn't very happy about it. So much so that he called Bogdan.

On the man's private phone, too.

Something else for the doctor to bitch about the next time he and Vaslav stood face to face. Like it would make a real difference to the fact that not once had Vaslav promised the man to be a model patient.

Vaslav wasn't *any* or every man. He was him, and that meant he expected more of those around him accordingly. Including from his doctors. Or rather—his *doctor*, at the moment. Dealing with one medical professional was already asking a lot from Vaslav's thin patience and non-existent trust. Neither of which he had much to offer to begin with. Life certainly had a way of keeping him on his toes. That, or the universe was having a good laugh at his expense.

"I could write you a script for something to help with the lack of appetite," Bogdan had said that morning on the phone when Vaslav called at what the doctor grumbled was an ungodly, unacceptable hour—it was nearly *nine*.

To be fair, Vaslav thought Bogdan should have counted himself lucky that he didn't drive to the other side of Moscow to pay the doctor a personal visit when his migraine had still been a solid fucking ten on the pain scale.

No, he absolutely did *not* want more pills, because really, he didn't even want to take the ones he was already on. Bogdan's final suggestion for the unfortunate new symptom related to the medications?

"Get some dank weed, then."

If not for the subsequent phone call Vaslav received less than an hour after Bogdon hung up on him, he might have actually made that trip to the doctor's private residence. Alas, life had once again decided to step in the way of letting Vaslav release his

50

rage. A little more for him to bottle up instead.

Because that wasn't concerning *at all.*

Despite his spiraling, hyper-focused thoughts on his doctor keeping him from finishing the property sketch on his desk, Vaslav had yet to forget the time. He clocked the goddamn time again only to find he still wasn't pleased with what stared back. Barely ten minutes had passed since he last checked.

"Oh—you weren't hungry?"

The soft question from the den's open doorway reminded Vaslav that he wasn't alone in the large house no matter what it felt like to him when Vera was gone. Strange how things like that worked …

"I tried," he said lamely to a waiting Mira. It wasn't a lie. The sandwich had one bite from each triangular end, and the bowl of the stainless-steel spoon still held the remnants of the red soup's broth at the very bottom. He opted not to mention how those two bites and one spoonful had tased like what he imagined cardboard did.

The taste wasn't Mira's fault. She *could* cook.

He gestured to the tray of untouched food, saying, "Go ahead and take it."

He could have called Mira back an hour ago when she first brought the tray in, but the food had been yet another distraction for Vaslav to keep from watching the clock on and off. Something else to focus his irritation and annoyance on that was visible and tangible. Not to mention, *explainable.*

"Give the sandwich to Marrow," Vaslav said as Mira entered the den to remove the tray. "Better not to waste it, no?"

"Oh, don't you worry," Mira assured. "That dog's scrap bowl is never empty."

She paused, then, and gave Vaslav a smile before picking up the tray and adding, "Well, until he gets to the bowl, that is."

The pup was more prone to eat scraps in the winter months, and often stayed inside the rear hallway to get out of the cold. Vaslav wasn't the only beating heart on the property with a mood about the changing seasons.

"Right," Vaslav replied absentmindedly.

His distraction did not go unnoticed.

"Did the car service call?" Mira asked.

Vaslav would like to say he was surprised that Mira had picked the right raw nerve causing his current disconnect and surly disposition, but that would be a lie. Anyone who had any real look at his day to day knew the massive difference Vera's presence made to his mood and life. Even if he didn't say as much, he didn't have to. She spoke for herself.

"They did," he eventually confirmed.

"Mrs. Pashkov is on her way home?" Mira brightened at the prospect of Vera's later arrival to the estate, but it faded the second she realized Vaslav hadn't shown the same excitement. Yet, she didn't prod for more.

"She's on her way home," Vaslav murmured, eyeing the clock again but not adding anything extra to the news. After all, he still hadn't decided how to feel about it. That was entirely Vera's doing, too.

Well ...

Vera got her weekend trip with her friend and mother before a very busy week that would lead into the Avdonin's departure from the country. He gave her that, at least. What happened when she got home, however, was an entirely different matter.

"Mira," Vaslav called at the woman's back as she headed out of the den, "could you make me a pot of tea?"

Even if it ended up tasting like cardboard, too—oh, well. It was something in his stomach. At the moment, he was running on nothing which couldn't be helping his souring mood.

*

"Are you … are you *ignoring me?*" Vera asked quietly.

Had Vaslav not been listening for the pitter-patter of Vera's footsteps following him into the walk-in closet attached to their bedroom, then she might have been able to sneak up on him. In any case, he had heard her, and she wasn't entirely wrong in her accusation.

"Only partly," Vaslav replied as he pulled open the middle doors of the wall-length wardrobe. "I'm also very fucking tired."

And ready to go to bed after a hot shower.

Honesty was the best policy. Even if his honesty caused a sheet of sad confusion to fall over Vera's pretty features when he glanced back at her. Oh, well for her. It wouldn't change. He'd started this thing out between them the same way. Constantly spilling his raw, unfiltered thoughts between them for her to absorb whether she liked it or not.

Awkward, painful, or otherwise.

He laid it bare.

He'd truly believed that he expected the same from her. That was the only problem with love. It assumed too much.

"How many hours did that take you to figure out?" Vaslav asked while he yanked out a pair of cotton sleep pants and slammed the drawer shut after. "Four?"

Vera's gaze narrowed into slits from the closet's doorway. "You can't help it, can you?"

"What?"

"Being a prick. You can't help it."

Vaslav pulled in a hiss of air through his teeth, making it sound like he was considering her statement but really, it was all for show. "I can't even blame it on the pain right now, either."

He was just mad.

Yes, at her.

But not yet ready to tell her *why*.

All at once, the promise she'd shown to push back drifted away, and the sadness came back while Vera glanced down and picked at her fingernails. "If you didn't want me to go to the city for a couple of days, then why didn't you just say?"

"You're foolish if you think a trip away for a night and day is enough to make me not even want to look at you."

It made those handful of hours since she'd arrived home particularly difficult for them both, too. Where he would usually want her within his constant arm's reach as dinner was served and the evening's darkness turned into a cold, bottomless black, instead he kept an obvious distance. He outright refused to speak when she made any attempt at conversation when they were in the same room together. Silence could be his only companion when he, for the first time, was truly angry at Vera for something she alone did.

That sting?

It reminded him a hell of a lot of betrayal. Vaslav couldn't play that treacherous game. Not with his *wife*. He'd done that once and paid a terrible price.

Finally, Vera's backbone decided to make an appearance when she tipped her chin up and fire stared back in her eyes. He might have respected that on another day; a different time and dispute between them. Just not for this.

"Well, when you work up the balls to tell me what's got you in a mood," Vera told him, every challenging word she spoke pissing him off more and more, "then let me know. I'll be around." She turned away from the doorway, adding, "Maybe Mira needs help with something downstairs. Even washing floors at night would be better than standing here doing this with you."

That's how he knew—her secret was just that, a *secret*. She really didn't know what had him so angry with her. She'd done something out of his view and believed he wouldn't find out. Not surprisingly, it also made him think she didn't intend to tell him what she had tried to do, either.

Vaslav took his time following the path Vera had taken, and when he exited the walk-in closet, she was already all the way across the bedroom. Nearly to the opened doors leading to the master's sitting room.

He could have let her go. His anger would only stretch on longer, making his bitterness worse, and the sting sharpen into something neither of them wanted.

Maybe he should have.

Instead, Vaslav asked, "Did you think the Roseville facility wouldn't inform me when my wife spent the morning making calls on my mother's behalf?"

Vera froze in the doorway, the skirt of the black dress she wore wishing around her calves until the silky fabric came to a stop. With a scoop neck in the back and front, he could see the way her shoulders and neck tensed as she toyed with her hands out of his view.

"First of all," she started.

Vaslav didn't care to play that game. "First of all, *nothing*. How did you even know where my mother was?"

"Mira mentioned something that made me curious."

Of course.

Vaslav didn't give away how the news landed unceremoniously at his feet. Besides, what Vera said next was far more interesting.

"But I found papers for a wire transfer in the den—"

"On my desk," Vaslav interjected, knowing already what she had to have found because it would be the only related thing in the house to the Roseville facility housing his unwell mother. That also explained how she had a number to call for the facility as it was listed at the top of the paperwork. "Were you looking for it?"

He wanted to clarify that point.

For his own reasons.

Vera let out weak, but still annoyed, laugh. "What difference does it make? And I didn't make a bunch of calls. Certainly not on her *behalf*," she spat over her shoulder at him. "It wasn't like that. I called the reception, and was put through elsewhere where I left a damn message."

"For her doctor."

"It's a psychiatric facility, Vaslav," Vera said.

His brow shot up. "Yes, that's usually where the mentally unwell find themselves when no one else can care for them, isn't it?"

"Is she?"

"What?"

"Mentally unwell," Vera returned. "Or did you just shove her there to keep her out of sight, and out of mind?"

Ah.

There it was.

All the little details that he didn't have to answer the whys in his mind. Those same questions that had plagued him since that morning when the doctor handling his mother's patient file at Roseville decided to call and inform him that a woman proclaiming to be his wife had left a message on his assistant's phone requesting a call back about Natalia Pashkova.

"The woman is where she needs to be," Vaslav settled on saying.

Vera's brow furrowed, but she kept watching him over her shoulder, seemingly determined not to drop his gaze. No matter the topic of conversation, or how she felt about it. "That doesn't really answer my question."

"I didn't realize you were owed one. She isn't *your* mother, after all."

"Good thing—right?" Vera asked quietly. "That's what everyone's told me who knows anything at all about her. You. Mira. Even Igor, although to his credit, he outright told me to be grateful I didn't know her face in a crowd."

"He's right."

"But is she unwell, or are you punishing her for

what she did to you?"

Wouldn't that be poetic?

Wouldn't it feel so fucking good?

"Isn't that what she deserves?" he asked back. "If I did?"

"I was only curious," Vera said, opting not to answer his question, but he didn't mind. "About her, mostly. I know things about her, stuff she's done to you, but I don't have a person to put a face to the name and deed. You know?"

"So ask for a fucking picture, *kisska*."

"Ask you," Vera hedged, "about *her*? History tells me I know better, thanks."

His fists clenched into tight balls. He couldn't deny that even standing there having this conversation about his mother with a woman who was nothing like Natalia, and deserved to be kept far away from her poison, took more effort than he wanted to give.

"I'll be the happiest on the day she dies," he admitted.

"I know," Vera returned softly. "I hear it, and I've heard it before."

Except she didn't yet *feel* it.

Not like he did deep in her chest, woven into her sinew, and constantly racing through her bloodstreams.

Not like him. Not yet.

She couldn't.

It was entirely possible that Vera didn't have the capability to feel hatred—not true, unabashed hatefulness like he did for his own mother. It also couldn't be ignored that she didn't experience the life he had under the harmful, violent hands of a mother like his, too.

That certainly shaped the child.

And their love.

"She's not like yours," he told her. "She won't be like Claire. She won't make you feel safe, or loved, or even *wanted*. They are not the same, and if all you need is to know that, I'll make it happen."

Vera still didn't move from her position just inches from the bedroom's doorway. "What does that mean—you'll make it happen?"

"It means exactly what I said. You didn't need to sneak an attempt at a phone call to her doctor for that. Did you at least put the transfer papers away somewhere?"

"Why didn't *you*?" Vera threw back.

They both knew why. It was how she used it as a weapon—even if it was only words—that cut the deepest. Maybe it was just defensiveness that pushed her to do it, but he had to remind himself that Vera's desire to understand all the facets of his life and mind stemmed from the fact that she loved him, and was always trying to find a way to help. She meant no harm, but that very sentiment took on a whole new meaning for Vaslav with Vera when it did, in fact, hurt.

That's why it stung like betrayal.

It wasn't.

So why did it still have to sting?

"It's not as if I made a hundred copies and sent them to every name in the phone book, Vas."

"Why don't you go find Mira like you said," he settled on saying to the waiting woman by the door. "She'll enjoy a second pair of hands to help wash the floors. She likes her work more when there's someone to talk to."

If anything, he thought that made his desire to end the conversation clear.

6.

"Can you believe that idiot?" Vaslav asked, ranting to himself as he crossed the bedroom floor and headed for the bathroom with a garment bag swinging from his grip. "*Cashmere,* he says. Better suited for *retirement!*"

"Who or what now?"

After a half of a week with little talk between Vaslav and Vera, spent mostly avoiding one another other than meals, he had started to think she was simply going to move her belongings right down the hall to the small guest bedroom. He'd woken up every morning alone, so what was he to think?

Not that he blamed her.

He did need the space.

"Are you using the drain as an ashtray?" Vaslav asked as he came to a stop just beyond the master bathroom's threshold.

Vera barely glanced up from the opened book spread open on her bare thighs before she went right back to reading. Perched on a wooden foot stool in the open shower, she pulled another drag from a lit, white-filtered cigarette before extending her arm over the drain, and flicking a non-existent ash over top. Her actions spoke for themselves.

"Are we acting like you haven't been hotboxing the bathroom all week with that weed Igor brought for you, then?" Vera asked as she flipped a page in her book. "Because the exhaust fan in here is better than anywhere else in the house?"

As her fingers rapped a beat against the next page of her book, Vera peered up and across the room at him with an almost saccharine smile. Not entirely true, but he wouldn't call her on it. "For the record, though, it still doesn't help with the smell. Mira agreed."

Dammit.

It irked him more than anything that she was able to call him out on his recent cannabis use without a hint of judgement or even annoyance, all the while, acting as if she hadn't asked it at all.

Nude, mind you. Oh, yeah, he forgot to mention that part.

Well, not entirely.

The silk robe she wore fell over her dainty shoulders but remained open on both ends, hanging like a thin sheet around her hips and the stool. White like the simple cotton panties she wore, the rest of her chest and front was bare. Nonetheless, the robe offered no shield for her naked breasts, and he found it particularly hard to look away when she was practically a tease sitting there like that just out of his reach. With one foot resting to the tile floor, and the other perched higher on the bottom rung of the stool, she didn't seem concerned with her lack of clothes.

Or the place she sat.

Not to mention, him.

"The weed helps with my appetite," he informed.

Vera didn't act shocked at the news, but he didn't care either way. The fact that the cannabis did help was what really mattered, so whoever disliked the smell could kick fucking rocks all the way to the lake for all he gave a damn.

"You could share it once in a while," she pointed out, peeking up at him through her dark lashes.

He might consider it.

Except he had other things on his mind.

"Is the book that good?" he asked.

Vera didn't reply.

"The cigarette, then?"

Vera did sigh at that question. "You've got me up to one a day, now. It's becoming a problem."

He scoffed. "*Me?* How did I do it?"

"Was there a problem with your suit?" Vera flipped another page, but Vaslav was almost one hundred percent sure she hadn't actually read the previous pages before doing so. "It's too late to get it fixed, right? Mira said it was sent in from the city last night."

She took another drag from the cigarette that was only half gone. From the point he'd woken up and did his business in the bathroom before running downstairs to grab the suit that had been delivered the night before, she somehow managed to find her way into his bathroom to light the tiny white stick and surprise him.

And he wasn't sure *why*. Vera had been all too content with leaving him to his own devices earlier in the week. He hadn't expected today to be any different.

Becoming bedmates with the opposite sex was one thing, but housemates was another monster altogether. Vaslav could count the number of women he'd lived with over his lifetime on one hand with a finger to spare. As his mother and Mira had been two of the women he lived under the same roof with, he hadn't shared a bed with them. Obviously. Irina, on the other hand, had seemed to take over every available square inch of his life and home that she could the second he let her do it. A strong woman with an equally strong will to ingratiate her ways and expectations on her husband, he'd adored her too much to refuse her anything. Not to mention, the sex after the fights had been fantastic.

Vera was not the same.

Not that he expected her to be, really.

Her things took up less space in their mutual closet than his own did. Tidiness certainly wasn't an issue because for her, everything had a place, and it went in that place when she was done with it. The woman could even set an alarm and roll out of bed, get ready for her day, and never once disturb his pitiful sleep while she did it.

Vera didn't complain, either. It wasn't as if she moved into Vaslav's home *expected* to behave a certain way or do those things—that was just how she seemed to be, and he liked it, frankly. He liked that for the most part, she didn't get in the way, but at the same time, was a companion he hadn't realized he needed all along. It made their fresh marriage and days feel less strange, if that was possible. New things brought changes he didn't manage well, but somehow she swept into his home like a permanent fixture that hadn't left.

Or perhaps the universe had finally given him something worth the many sacrifices he'd paid over his lifetime in the form of a woman he couldn't even hate if he tried. Especially when he was mad at her.

He blamed her for that, too.

"He told me to wear a cashmere sweater under the blazer," Vaslav said, settling on being the one who broke the silence between the two.

"Who?" Vera asked.

"My tailor."

"Did you ask for a shirt—"

"No, I have plenty. His advice, on the note taped to the pocket, was to opt for a cashmere sweater instead of a standard button down. Apparently, that'll better reflect my retirement. My *retirement*, Vera."

"And you're annoyed because—"

"He knows about my retirement!"

To start.

Vaslav had other issues with the note left by the tailor he preferred, like the fact that the man felt comfortable enough to leave a personal note for him to begin with. But that was an issue he could deal with on a different day.

This one's schedule was full.

Taking her time to fold the book in her lap closed, Vera carefully set the paperback book down to the tiled floor of the shower stall next to the mug full of coffee that didn't appear to have been touched yet. "Didn't I talk to him for an entire hour on Monday about the mood you wanted for your suit? *Not* formal, more casual. A muted black—warm for the weather."

"And?" Vaslav asked sharply.

Vera tilted her head to the side, unwavering in her calm disposition even as his worsened right before her eyes. "You mentioned, more than loud enough for him to hear, that it was the last time you planned to be seen with *vory* in public. Your words, not mine or his."

He hadn't realized she was still on the phone with the tailor when he made that comment because she wasn't even supposed to take the call to begin with. She conveniently forgot to mention that part of the story. Either way, he'd let her handle it when the last thing he'd needed was a half hour conversation on the phone when his skull felt like it was splitting open. Who cared about hemlines and thread color when his brain could explode at any fucking second?

"He must have put it together himself, and thought he'd pass on something helpful for today," Vera added with a small shrug. "What harm does that do? I thought you wanted news to spread. Who's to say it isn't?"

Of course, she just had to make sense.

That didn't mean he had to like it.

"It's not that important of a day," Vaslav muttered. "Not so much so that my personal tailor needed to put his input in on it, no?"

Vera didn't call him on the lie, and he would never say it, but he was grateful for her silence. It *was* a significant day. Definitely for the men involved, and partly for him, too. While the men in power would have their moment, in the grand scheme of the day's events, his part might only seem like a passing second.

That second would still mean a lot.

Every choice he had made in the past year accumulated to the proverbial passing of a torch in a public setting, and he hadn't really thought that much about it, if he were being honest. Which was unlike Vaslav who usually spent more time than he should obsessively overthinking almost everything.

Whatever.

This retirement business was easier to manage if he just let shit happen the way it was meant to. That included him taking a step back—no dirty hands, no making plans. If he had no skin in the game, and he pulled no strings, he was less of a threat in a way.

Or so he was told.

Vaslav didn't know if he believed it.

Vera continued her quiet observance of Vaslav as he headed deeper into the well-lit bathroom. Hanging the garment bag with his new suit on a hook, he then yanked open a drawer on the vanity to find the toiletry bag he kept inside. He spent the next couple of minutes spreading out the items he planned to use to get ready for the day while Vera finished her cigarette in the shower stall. Once she had done, and had sprayed the ashes down the drain, she tossed the butt to the toilet and flushed it. Lastly, she removed the stool from the stall and replaced it against the far wall. She lingered behind him in the reflection of the mirror as he trimmed his beard along his jawline with a pair of stainless steel scissors.

"Are you going with cashmere?" she asked.

"Should I?" he asked back.

"It's just clothing, Vas."

"Right," he returned. "And it's just another day, Vera."

Which wasn't at all true.

They both knew it, too.

"Well, it is comfortable," she said. "Warm, too."

"*Mmm.*"

His noncommittal grunt pulled a tiny grin from the woman behind him in the mirror. He dared to grin back, and didn't regret the choice when her lips split with a wider smile.

All those days of silence between them while he worked through how he felt about what she had done regarding his mother were for nothing when she smiled at him. The clouds in the sky could have parted with the rays and voice of God coming through, and it wouldn't have made one single damn difference to Vaslav in that second.

It was sickening, really. Except he wouldn't change a thing about it.

"I have a dress—grey, you saw it before. We could match."

He knew which one she meant. Loose sleeves, body-contouring, and a treat to enjoy the sight of her wearing the sweater dress.

"I do have a grey sweater," he admitted. "We can match without saying we are, yes?"

"Sure, if that's what you need to get dressed and leave this house today." Vera nodded. "I'll wear the grey dress, and find your sweater?"

Setting the scissors next to the sink, Vaslav scrubbed a hand down his jaw, brushing away the stray hairs he'd soon rinse off.

"All of this," he muttered, "for five minutes on the side of the street."

The comment stopped Vera from turning away to leave the bathroom.

"Five minutes?" she asked. "I thought we were having dinner with my parents in the city before they fly out tonight?"

Actually, he'd told her they would see her parents—and Igor—around dinnertime at a restaurant in downtown Moscow, and spend the night in the city after. He hadn't specified whether or not they would also join the meal but that was never in his plans.

After all, he'd made himself clear to Igor about their transition of power and how Vera could be used. If Igor wanted to initiate Vaslav's retirement and flex his new control by starting with a mutually beneficial agreement with an American Bratva boss on the trade of a significant stock of weapons, then so be it. The fact that the American boss also happened to be Vera's father presented a viable story to the rest of the organization that could be told without Vaslav needing to be a part of the conversation.

After all, he was trying to step away from said organization. He shouldn't *be* a part of the conversation in any real way at all. Wasn't that the point?

"Vas, what about dinner with my parents?" Vera asked again.

"Something came up," he said.

It wasn't a lie.

Not entirely.

Glancing over his shoulder, he found Vera still lingering in the doorway of the bathroom, not entirely ready to leave, it seemed. To be frank, he didn't want her to go, either. Even a few days of time, space, and silence was a little much for him.

At least, when he wanted her. God knew he *always* wanted her.

"You'll still get a chance to say your goodbyes," Vaslav added.

Vera's smile faded, but she nodded nonetheless. "Okay. So what else came up that's so important?"

Oh, that?

Vaslav shrugged. "That's a surprise."

Vera did a double take of him as if she hadn't heard him right the first time. "You got me ... a surprise?" she hedged. The barely contained curiosity in her voice also shone in her bright eyes. "The man who barely wanted to look at me all week—never mind *touch* me—has done something to *surprise* me?"

"Why do you say it like that?"

"Like what?"

He didn't know how to explain the way she'd twisted the word, saying surprise first like it was a good thing and then warping it the second time so that it was clear she understood he was being misleading. Vera was picking up on his tricks quicker than he expected her to.

At the mirror, he let her see his gaze travel from the simple cotton panties—bikini style—she wore up her bare chest before locking their stares together. "Is that why you're practically naked in here when you know I'm getting up and around and ready for this shitshow today? Were you trying to seduce me?"

If he hit a nerve, she didn't know it. In fact, her sly smile only stroked the heat that had been growing deep in his gut from the moment he walked into the bathroom and saw her perched half-naked on a stool while she smoked a cigarette and read.

"I don't need to try," she returned.

She wasn't wrong, but Vaslav doubted he was off the mark, either. He'd yet to mention the sleek bullet vibrator—clean, and seemingly out of batteries—she let him find in the guest bedroom under her pillow that morning. Yes, he'd actually had to look to find it, but Vera wasn't the type to leave her bed messy after she left it in the mornings; which was part of the reason he stumbled on it in the first place.

Why had he gone looking for her before starting his day? For the first morning ever since they woke up in the same bed together as husband and wife, she had made good and sure he heard her running through her morning routine. Except by the time he was up and around to do his own, she had slipped out of their master's connected suites and back to the guest bedroom.

Or so he thought when he went looking.

He could call her on the lie—she *was* trying something. Even if it was subtle to grab his attention. Knowing she'd be wearing a particular dress he liked for the day only added to the strain on his thin self-control.

Now just wasn't the time. Not with a day like theirs ahead. A pity for them both, really.

Vaslav turned on the cold water tap, and thrust his hands under the stream to gather a cupful he could use to splash under his jaw and down his throat. Before he did, he asked her, "You want what you want, don't you? Wasn't that what you told me?"

He planned to give it to her. Even if it had made him mad at first.

Vera's brow knotted in the middle, voicing her otherwise silent confusion. "I want a lot of things. I'm not sure what you mean."

"My mother. You're curious. A face to the name— isn't that what you told me, *da*?"

He gave her studious, unruffled attitude credit. The fact that he hadn't as much as whispered about his mother since the evening he confronted Vera with her secret phone call meant she should have been surprised to hear him bring it up so frankly now.

"You're right," he told her, knowing how cruel his flat tone could be, "it's not a good surprise. Natalia barely passes as tolerable on her good days. Sorry about your luck."

"Are you telling me we're going to see your mother?"

Wasn't that what she wanted?

"That sweater I mentioned, the grey one," Vaslav said, changing the conversation altogether, "would you go find it for me now? I feel like I'm already late to get a start on this fucking day."

Better to just get it all over with.

The good and bad.

Vera stared hard at him in the reflection of the mirror, but he was careful to avoid her gaze even as it followed him when he headed for the tower of rolled, fresh black towels on a stand in the corner by the shower. "I thought you didn't want anything to do with her? Didn't we just spend a week ignoring each other because you don't want me to even speak about her like she exists, or wh—"

"I want you to understand, *kisska.*"

And then he bet she would never ask about Natalia ever again. Some lessons, this one in particular, had to be learned firsthand. He'd never been a terribly good teacher.

7.

Two city blocks away from the restaurant—where Vera would get her very brief chance to say goodbye to her mother and father before they attended a dinner that would start a larger conversation in the Russian criminal underworld—Vaslav finally decided to break the stretch of silence that had accompanied them since Dubna's rural back roads. His silence, to her at least, was worse than even his anger. At least when he voiced his distress and displeasure, she had something to work with. Silence was nothing more than a void of emptiness, and it left her entirely cold.

Except she hadn't heard him properly. Distracted by her thoughts as she yet again mulled over how to apologize for something she didn't regret doing, Vera turned away from the window as the white Rolls-Royce slowed to a stop at a red light.

"What did you say?" Vera asked.

A chuckle answered her back.

Vera wasn't sure what to make of that. "What's

funny?"

His gaze slid her way while something akin to a smirk tugged at the corner of his scarred mouth. "It's not like you to not pay attention, Vera."

"No offense, but you weren't exactly a great conversationalist after this morning in the bathroom, Vas."

He arched a brow and tilted his head her way in some semblance of a nod like he was non-verbally agreeing with her statement.

Vera shrugged. "And let me say, silence is the best way to make a person feel wanted. Can't forget that, right?"

Her sarcasm practically oozed, but she didn't tamper it for a second. She needed something—literally anything else—from this man except his silence. Maybe then it would make her apology easier.

Even if she didn't deserve easy.

Ahead of them, the light remained bright, and red.

Vaslav glanced her way. "Is that how you've felt all week?"

"What?"

"Is that what you *thought*—that my silence means I don't want you? You didn't feel wanted?"

She wasn't expecting his question, and she had to drop his gaze to consider how she wanted to respond. He didn't miss her blatant avoidance if the way his hands tightened on the leather steering wheel was any indication. A vehicle he wasn't supposed to drive outside of Dubna's limits if at all possible to keep it untraceable and private.

Apparently, after today, the Rolls wouldn't return to the estate. At least, not looking the way it currently did. Vaslav hadn't offered more information in that regard, and Vera wasn't that attached to the car to prod for more details.

"Well?" he asked, sharper that time. "Is that how it made you feel?"

She didn't answer him.

History taught her not to.

Vera wasn't a sucker for punishment, but Vaslav was the type of man who didn't mind delivering it if warranted. She didn't need him to point out how pitiful or weak it might make her to say his continued silent treatment had done nothing but make her spend nights alone with a tear-stained pillow as her bed companion.

Just because it was true didn't mean he needed to say it. It wouldn't change what it meant, either. Or that sometimes, that love still growing between them, well, it hurt.

"Vera."

She kept her eyes locked on the streetlight that changed to green when he murmured her name a second time. "You've got to go—it's green."

"Fuck the light. Look at me."

She still didn't.

The truck behind their car blew the horn, which only prompted Vaslav to lay on his in response. His hand flew out the six-inch crack where he'd rolled his window down during the drive to wave the middle finger while he let out a string of Russian expletives at the driver behind them. Perhaps the older, rusted vehicle behind them wasn't willing to get into a tussle with someone driving a vehicle like theirs because the truck was quick to pull around their vehicle and blow through the light when the oncoming traffic wasn't in the way.

"*Suka—bitch*," he said under his breath as the truck moved into the intersection.

Other vehicles who came up behind them at the light did the same thing. Only one or two blew their horns as they passed the Rolls.

Vera tried not to look like something wounded and sad when she turned to finally meet Vaslav's stare when he muttered, "We're not moving one goddamn inch until you look at me, *kisska*."

"I know it's silly and stu—"

"I didn't mean to make you feel like that," Vaslav interrupted, taking her off guard with the way his tone softened. The breath she hadn't realized she'd been holding came out of her chest with a hard woosh. The same man who had once mocked her for admitting that dancing made her sometimes cry now scowled beside her with his unhappiness at the thought of her not feeling wanted by him. That was a wave of emotional whiplash that she really wasn't ready to ride.

"*Come here.*"

The light was still green.

Vera just blinked.

Dumbly.

"*Now*," Vaslav uttered as he reached for her. He must have kept one foot heavy on the break because their car didn't roll an inch as he closed the distance between them over the center console separating their seats. All over again, her lungs burned with a need to breathe, but it wasn't because she was holding the air in this time. His arms wrapped under the white fox fur coat that he'd produced for her before they left the house earlier.

A surprise that had delighted her.

Except that joy was also stained with everything left unsaid between them, too. She couldn't forget that. At least, she didn't until he swallowed her in his bar-like arms, burying her face into his chest while his hands wandered from her shoulders to her lower back.

Another horn blared while the Rolls rocked from the speed of a vehicle racing around theirs. It didn't register to Vaslav or Vera, and the kiss he placed to the crown of her head was all she needed to keep her firmly in place.

She even grabbed fistfuls of his sweater. Thin, soft cashmere that she had pulled out of his closet for him and picked out her own dress for the day accordingly.

Little things, sure.

But they meant everything to her.

He'd made it all the more difficult for her by not allowing her those things—as little and simple as they might be—over the past few days, and Vera had not managed it well. *He* didn't tell her to leave their bed. She did that because silence alone was better than silence with him beside her.

She only noticed that the light had switched back to red at the intersection when Vaslav had urged her face higher with his hands under her chin while he nuzzled along her throat with his soft, warm lips. She didn't try to calm the galloping beat of her heart that he could surely feel when he lingered on her pulse point before his hands cupped her chin. He tipped her head back further, offering him ample room to drop a kiss, firm and lingering, against her lips.

"That is not how you should ever feel," he told her. "My words are weapons, and sometimes silence is the mercy."

Vera's lower lip trembled from the emotions she failed to quell. "Okay."

As lame as it was, she couldn't think of anything else to say. He pressed another kiss against her mouth before she could get another word out. Somehow, she found the courage to speak the words that she should have said many nights ago when he made it clear she had crossed a line for him.

"I'm sorry," she whispered, the words breathless as fast between a rising hiccup and water welling in her eyes.

She didn't want to cry.

There wasn't even a *reason*.

"I know you are," he murmured.

All at once, he pulled away to resume his previous position in the driver's seat. One of his hands stayed firm on her thigh, though, high underneath the hem of her skirt where he could grab tight enough that she was sure his fingerprints would be left behind by the time he let go.

She didn't mind.

Yet, his voice was still cold when he stared out the window to wait for the light overhead to once again turn green, and said, "But after today, Vera, you'll know why you should be sorry, too."

"I know why."

Perfectly well.

Her wrongdoing was clear.

Vaslav sighed. "No, *kisska*, you won't until you meet her. Trust me on that."

*

Vera had just enough time to settle her emotions,

and blink away what tears might remain, before Vaslav pulled the Rolls off on the brick-lined entry drive of a restaurant with wide bay windows featuring heavy, black drapery. She hadn't even properly read the name on the sign, only partly snow-covered, and their vehicle came to slow stop under the towering car port.

"Igor will have only recently given your parents the news that we won't join them as originally planned," Vaslav said. "Try to act like you were recently told the same. We're a passing moment in this day, Vera, and for good reason."

While his hand had left her thigh to shift the vehicle into park, it wasn't long before his palm found its former home ... still warm from how he left it. Only this time, his hand went even higher under the skirt of her grey cashmere dress with a gentle rub that had her breath catching hard in her lungs.

"You say that like this was always the plan," she replied. "Was it—or was the chance to visit your mother today just a convenient excuse?"

He shrugged.

She tried not to glower. "At least tell me the truth."

Vaslav's icy gaze drifted from Vera's face to somewhere behind her through the window. She didn't turn to look for what he saw, but she didn't need to when he explained, "Important people will hear interesting things over the course of your parents' dinner with Igor. How long it takes word to travel about those things is the only real variable to what will happen in the end. I've chosen to remove myself from the equation as much as possible, but that might not make you or I safe."

He offered that information to her as if she already

had the final picture of the puzzle he'd put together in his own head regarding his retirement, and Igor's subsequent takeover. Because she didn't actually have the image he seemed to think she did, Vera tried to look at the situation from his point of view.

What must it be like to have to constantly contemplate the plans and intentions of those around you? As malfeasance and violence waited in every wing. In that case, wouldn't everyone and anything look like a threat?

"Igor doesn't have the legacy of the men who came before him. He doesn't stand in the middle of the room as a warning to far worse men. I did," Vaslav said, his stare falling back to hers as he offered an almost awkward smile. "And I still had four assassination attempts—two while my mother had me locked in the asylum. Believe me when I say the facility that's housing her crazy ass is far kinder than the one she locked me into. At the very least, they might help."

Vera was not ready for that dump of trauma he spilled into her lap. It was a terrible time considering he nodded at something over her shoulder, and immediately added, "There's your mother and father coming out. Be mindful someone could hear, and if you sleep down the hall for one more goddamn night, I will chain you to our bed for the next month. I'll need the extra warmth for the next bit. It gets terribly cold in Dubna, *kisska*."

Her mouth popped open instantly. Vaslav grinned with a playful wink that made her jaw snap shut with an audible crack.

"You're always doing that to me—at the worst times, too," she muttered, turning to open the car door while heat flooded her cheeks.

"Relax," he called at her back, "I'm not even getting out of the car."

That news only helped a little.

Vera wouldn't have to deal with the physical effects of Vaslav being near, touching and surveying her while she said her goodbyes to her parents. Instead, she only had to manage the mental lashing his lustful promise left her with while his chuckles chased her out of the vehicle.

"Promises, promises," she taunted before shutting the door on his deepening laughter.

For the split second before she turned around to face her parents, who were already calling her name, the relief that swept through Vera left her almost light on her feet. She hadn't realized how much she missed his playful, *too*-suggestive banter keeping her on her toes. Yet another thing that had been missing from her prior days.

"I would have come out to Dubna again had I known we weren't going to at least have dinner before we flew out," Claire said.

Reminding Vera of why this quick greeting and departure felt all too bittersweet.

"I know, Ma. Stuff … happened," she said lamely.

"Everything's okay, right?" Claire asked.

"Sure it is," Demyan told his wife. "Look, she's smiling."

Vera's grin bloomed wider as she fully faced her parents under the car port. The white fox fur did well to keep her safe from the cold. Every blustery wind brought with it spiraling flakes under the roof as Vera opened her arms for her oncoming mother.

Somehow, Claire still managed to swallow her

daughter whole with her hug although she wore a thinner, black tweed coat.

"I'm sorry we can't come to dinner," Vera said.

Claire pulled away from the hug with a shrug. "It's okay."

"It's not," Demyan interjected before his wife could say more, giving Vera a pointed look before he added, "but you did promise us a visit stateside in the spring, yes?"

Had she?

Demyan noticed the confused surprise in his daughter's face, but still encompassed her in his familiar, warm hug. "By the lake, remember?" Once he poked the memory, it did float to the surface, and the fact that she had only said it to stop them from fighting. Whether it was feasible now mattered little, though. Quieter, he told her, "I'm holding you to that."

If she were being honest, lately, it seemed like the whole universe held her to a lot.

8.

"Name?" the security guard at the stone gatehouse asked.

"Vaslav Pashkov."

As the man behind the fiberglass window with the speaker turned away to face what Vaslav suspected was a computer screen, he checked the woman in the passenger seat of the Rolls. Vera, more interested in the stonework of the tall wall that hid and protected the property within, didn't notice Vaslav looking.

"And the lady?" asked the man in the window.

That caught Vera's attention, and her head swung in their direction. Her gaze darted between Vaslav in the driver's seat, and the security guard who hadn't acknowledged her otherwise until that very moment.

"Vera Av—Pashkov," she was quick to correct.

It made Vaslav smile.

But only a little.

He couldn't help it, even as Vera looked to him after her mistake with an awkward smile, he didn't provide more emotion in his expression than he already had. This was how he needed to deal with the entire day, frankly, and nothing would change that. There was no other way to manage the hollow emptiness and rage his mother induced the closer he was to her person except to shut it all off.

It helped with the rage, anyway. The empty hollowness was another matter altogether.

"You're good to go," the security muttered, passing back Vaslav's identification card that he'd first handed over when he pulled up to the gatehouse for the Roseville facility. Along with the card was a slip of paper printed with their names, vehicle identification, and a tri-digit number. In his flat gray uniform, the guard pointed at the gate just two feet ahead of the chrome grill of the Rolls, and explained, "You park in the spot with the matching number. Check in at the gate when you leave."

"*Spasibo*," Vaslav replied.

The man only nodded before his finger jammed into the speaker, causing it to buzz and crackle before it shut off. A louder, but similar, noise began as the gate started to slide sideways ahead of their car.

"Careful place," Vera noted quietly. "Is there security at the front doors, too?"

"And throughout the grounds and building. You'll never not see one, according to their information sheet. Not to mention, the fucking cameras everywhere. Could do without that, if I'm being honest."

"Do they need all of it, though?"

Vaslav's hand tightened around the wheel. "I'd say so. Everyone from the criminally insane to the last president's wife are holed up here. I heard she comes and goes, however. Apparently, he's got her a permanent suite she uses that she likes. It comes with a hefty price tag, no?"

"Really?"

"If we're sharing, yes, I paid a good amount for Natalia's treatment and time here. Not that it guarantees anything at this point. I'm now paying more for this," he said, gesturing at the front windshield and what waited beyond it, "than I was to keep her the fuck away from me."

He peeked her way, but Vera's attention had already been snagged by the two-by-two-foot brass plaque on a tall sign with Roseville's information spelled out for arriving guests. Once they were beyond the sign and gate, and the looming face of the Roseville facility was in view beyond the snowy entrance grounds, Vera couldn't quite seem to settle in her seat.

She played with her nails, and then squirmed in her spot. She even unbuckled her seatbelt before Valsav could pull off on the paved, but icy, drive into the designated carports for staff or visitors.

He wanted to point out her nerves and ask about them—and *would*, as soon as he found their designated parking spot among the many rows of vehicles.

Vera filled him in before he could do either of those things. "You mean, what I'm paying, right?"

She didn't say it with malice or sarcasm. Just an honest question with facts to back it up because he was there the night the paperwork was faxed through, and she signed her name on every line he told her to.

Each one for a different account. Banks, properties, and investments. All of it now belonged to her at the end of the day. Of course, he still had access to the money—or rather, he was able to handle the money and move it how he pleased with minimal limits, hence his ability to deal with his mother's medical care, but that was only for practical purposes.

He had no intention of draining any account behind Vera's back, or doing untoward things with the money that could cause her issues in the future. That wasn't the point. His wealth was simply one more thing he chose to let go of—in a way—for the sake of his retirement. There was nothing to take; nothing to ruin if it wasn't actually his. The accountant who previously handled his dirty money and protected it likely appreciated the constant threat that followed them simply by being attached to Vaslav's money in a tangible way.

Not that it mattered now.

"If it helps," he settled on saying as he pulled into the spot with the number that matched his slip spray painted to the brick wall their car now faced, "it'll probably work out to the same at the end of the year if I factor in all the money I shovel out to clean up my mother's messes. Her allowance was like a ..." He considered how he wanted to work that, trailing off long enough for Vera to cock an eyebrow in question. "A base pay, yeah?"

"And the rest is what?"

Vaslav chuckled dryly. "A consequence for my repeated stupidity."

Obviously.

He had no one to blame for the mess that was his mother except for himself, and perhaps that was the part of this entire situation that bothered Vaslav the most more than anything else. Had he simply dealt away with his mother decades ago when she was at the very height of her worst and most toxic behavior, then he could have saved a lot of people from a great deal of grief and trauma down the line. Starting with himself, rounding out around his first wife, and now …

Well, hindsight was what it was.

Vaslav glanced Vera's way who had yet to make a move to exit the vehicle even though he had turned off the engine. "I was told they're particular about keeping appointment times."

Vera nodded, but absentmindedly. Her fingernails, on the other hand, took the brunt of her anxiety. "Oh, okay. I guess we'd better—"

"What is it?" he asked. "You were willing to make personal calls, but now that we're here and making a proper visit, you don't want to meet your mother-in-law?"

She didn't appreciate his sarcasm if her scowl was any indication.

"I never said that," she returned just as fast.

"You're about to pick off that French manicure from your spa trip. You didn't have to say it, *kisska*. I'm not blind."

Vera's fidgeting stopped instantly, but her glower didn't lessen for even a second. "You know, all I really cared about was why she was here. You've come up with the rest all on your own, and I at least had the decency not to point it out."

Until now.

He heard what she didn't say.

If only it made a difference.

"Is that still all you care about?" he asked.

Vera shrugged. "If why means she *should* be here,

well—"

"After I cut off her financial support the month before we married, she had two unsuccessful suicide attempts. Both of which came on after her usual drinking binges, but the last one landed her in a psych ward in the city hospital. That's when I got called."

Or rather, Mira took the first message and then passed the information along. Vaslav never even had to speak to his mother to deal with the situation at hand. Roseville happened shortly after.

He never cared to find out how Natalia felt about the transfer, and if she had a clue about his involvement in getting her into Roseville, he couldn't say. Never mind the fact that until the doctors signed off on her file, she wouldn't be let out. That couldn't happen unless she was no longer a danger to herself or others. It took very little time in his mother's vicinity to learn she would always be those things in one way or another.

"Add a handful of personality and behavior disorders on top of her long-term alcoholism, and I can't think of a better place she's suited to be except here," Vaslav said.

As he reached for the inner door handle on the driver's side to exit the vehicle once and for all, Vera asked, "But how long will that be? Her stay here, I mean."

Vaslav shoved the car door open, muttering under his breath, "If I'm lucky, the rest of her damned life."

If his wife had heard his hateful comment, Vera didn't say.

Truth be told, he'd never been the one with a pocket full of luck, however, and he doubted the universe would pay him back in arrears now by starting with his mother. That just wasn't how this shit worked for him.

Leaning back in the opened door of the Rolls, he told Vera before he shut it, "Let's go. Not even Moscow's Beast gets a pass on a late appointment in hell. And say goodbye to the Rolls—I'll call for a driver to take us back to the city for the night."

Vera wasn't long scrambling out of the car after he shut the door. "Wait, you're just *leaving* the Rolls-Royce here? For good?"

He wasn't surprised that she hadn't forgotten his news about getting rid of the Rolls before they returned to Dubna. Vaslav admired the rear of the vehicle as Vera rounded the back to come and stand at his side. "It's been well-used."

Just not often.

And should someone come looking for him in a white Rolls—well, too bad for that poor fool.

"You can't just leave it parked here—aren't we supposed to check out with the same vehicle when we leave?" she asked him.

"They'll impound it."

Eventually, he'd be notified and it wouldn't change anything. Vaslav had no intention of retrieving the vehicle, and he didn't care what happened to it beyond the impound. Likely an auction to the highest bidder, and the government would absorb the profits made.

The loss didn't hurt.

"And what will we drive when a driver isn't a phone call away?" Vera questioned.

Cute, he thought. There would always be someone on call. Someone willing to take payment in the form of cold, hard cash that couldn't be traced to do his bidding. As long as he always had the money to pay.

But to answer her question …

"Christmas is only a couple of weeks away," he told Vera. "Don't be so impatient."

"My family never really celebrated Christmas."

"Right, non-practicing Jews." Vaslav shrugged under the weight of his thick tweed jacket. "I'm not all that concerned you might refuse the presents."

When did she ever refuse a gift from him?

Vera's lips lifted slightly at the edges, barely holding back her smile. "Now there's more than one?"

"I bet you were a kid that would have snooped under the tree, hmm?"

Vera playfully stuck out her tongue at that. At least her mood was better than it had been a few moments ago. Vaslav would take that as a win.

Besides, he was sure he could find something for them to do together while she waited for the present he'd had in the works since before they married. Hell, he had to do something with the stacks of money and gold bars in the safe under his den, didn't he?

New wheels seemed like a fine idea. He'd even teach her how to drive.

*

"For transparency's sake," the woman with a skin-tight cream-colored pencil skirt and matching blouse said from her wide-armed leather chair in the center of the room, "I feel like I should fill you in on a few things that have happened since your mother arrived here."

Doctor Nanessa Bovich had greeted Vaslav and Vera into her private office with kindness, and a request that they call her by her first name. Unless they were around staff, or patients. Partly policy, she'd explained, for professionalism and ethics within the facility. However, it was clear to Vaslav that the woman—who, at her mid-forties seemed to have given up on taming the grey streaks lining her messy curls that she piled high into a large bun—simply flicked the switch for her personality depending on which person was in the room. No doubt, because being Doctor Bovich every hour of every day was a taxing task in a place like this.

What things did she hear?

Or *see*?

He couldn't imagine spending eighty-hour weeks, or more, wrapped up in perfect professionalism and also keep his head straight on top of it. The fact that the woman still managed to slip in a personality that was her own amidst the clinical psychiatrist she had to be spoke to the woman's love for her profession, likely.

Dainty fingers, bare of jewelry or even nail polish, waved at the two sitting across from her on the couch. The gesture marked them, and her, clearly.

"We shouldn't even be doing this," she told them, nodding once while her sharp gaze widened a bit more for dramatic effect like it would impart to Vaslav and Vera just how significant that was. He didn't give a shit—when he paid in the range of a respectable home's worth monthly for private care, and Roseville was willing to sign off on it because they couldn't refuse a man with his significance and power, yes, he might abuse that.

They were stupid if they thought he wouldn't.

"And I don't mean just this private chat in my

office," Nanessa added quickly before Vaslav could open his mouth to tell the woman all the reasons why she needed to move on from this conversation. "But we'll get to that in a minute—Mr. Pashkov, I won't play these games with you. Your mother is far more than enough."

Vera stiffened beside him.

Vaslav, however, cracked a smile. "Already, huh?"

The way the doctor's thin lips tightened into an even thinner slit told Vaslav all he needed to know regarding how the woman felt about his mother.

"I understand that you have some influence with a few directors on the board, and a certain politician—"

"The president didn't even have to make a call," he returned just as fast.

The initial fight the doctor displayed deflated like her shoulders, as she broke their gaze with a defeated shake of her head. "This is not her first time in Roseville, sir."

Finally, Vera spoke up.

"How many times has she been committed at this facility?"

"Ten since the age of nine. It's an extensive file, Mrs. Pashkov."

"If I can call you Nanessa, I'd like to be given the same respect."

"I could have mentioned that," Vaslav noted quietly to his wife.

Vera glanced up at him where she sat at his side on the leather loveseat that matched the doctor's current chair. Between them, an ornately woven rug took the brunt of her tapping foot's beat. "Yeah, you could have."

There was a reason that Vaslav had been able to

easily—and quickly—get his mother handled in a way that she wouldn't fight too much. It was a system that had followed her since childhood. Not even long sleeves could hide the jagged layers upon layers of scar tissue that had started to creep down the centers of his mother's palms.

Every time, the same way.

The thing was, that tended to be a mode of suicide that worked well when done properly. Natalia always did, of course, but she also craved attention. She would die happily in it, in fact. So every attempt to die had come with the selfish cost of a witness to bear the brunt of her pain.

Was it twisted?

Sick?

Was she?

He needn't answer the obvious.

"What *matters*," Nannessa said strongly, breaking Vera and Vaslav's silent staring contest and his spiraling train of thoughts, "and that I'd like to get back to, was what I initially said. We shouldn't do this."

"It's already been done," Vaslav replied, unbothered and calm. "Here we are."

"I meant, a visit with your mother. Listen, you make my work weeks any harder than they already are, and I'll ship your mother's file to someone in the west wing. Bart said he wouldn't mind, and frankly, he said personally that neither would you. I don't *want* to do that though. So keep it in mind for the next couple of minutes, okay?"

The fact that she used the head director's first name, the highest member of a faculty panel that ran and handled the proceeds and profits of Roseville, meant they were close enough personally and professionally to do so. It led him to believe she was telling the truth, and her assumption about how he'd feel to have his mother sent to a twenty-four hour locked down ward wouldn't hurt his feelings a bit, either.

"I don't mind dealing with Natalia, if she thinks she's getting something over on you she's happy. That's like playing with babies for me," Nanessa said, almost smirking. "But she had another episode on Monday—snatched a safety knife from a cook's helper in the kitchen."

"Why would she ever be in the kitchen?" Vaslav questioned.

"I don't think that happened there," the woman hedged.

Ah.

Natalia's games never ended. Not even in the madhouse.

"What man was she conning?" Vaslav asked.

Nanessa sighed, shifting her legs one over the other modestly, but it still gave the uncomfortable truth away, and she smacked her tongue off her teeth. "He was new ... and young."

"And fired, I hope," Vera muttered.

Oh, good. She had been following along. Vaslav hated when people couldn't fill in the blanks to a simple damned conversation.

"And fired," the doctor agreed. "Anyway, since she's been here, Vaslav, she's clung to the cry of her injustice. To anyone who wants to listen, by the way. It's your fault; you've locked her up; her son is a monster."

All the while, Vaslav understood, making time to

manipulate a young employee into getting her something dangerous so she could do what she wanted with it. Even in her sixties, Natalia didn't miss a single beat.

"Where did she do it?" Vaslav asked. "That's why she got the knife, yeah?"

Nanessa frowned. "Alone in her room, actually."

Vaslav quieted at that statement.

Vera noticed. "Is that new, or something?"

He didn't answer right away, and the way the doctor's gaze flicked from Vera to his said she wouldn't tell the truth, either, unless perhaps he okayed it. Really, he just needed a second to think.

"She likes to make a scene," Vaslav said. "It's a ... thing."

With everyone.

And everything.

But that story would take time they simply didn't have, so he shrugged his shoulders under the weight of his jacket, and said, "She gets off on being vindictive and manipulative, but she's also mentally unwell in her own right and sometimes, that gets everything a little twisted."

"That's not a great explanation of ... well, what does it matter," Nanessa muttered with a wave of her hand. "The point is, I wanted you in my office first so I could explain why I don't want you to meet with your mother today. You're going to prove everything she already thinks is true to be what it is, and that can't be helpful to anyone. Not when Monday, before this last knife incident, was the last time she even mentioned your name that anyone's heard."

"So she's on to another con."

Some emotional manipulation or otherwise,

perhaps even to convince the medical staff around her that she was getting better. Or was ready to try. He wouldn't put that above his mother because it wasn't the first time she'd tried it—never mind succeeded. Either way, his empathy and trust for her were practically nil.

Nonetheless, Roseville was the best place for that particular brand of his mother's fun. They knew her history, and games, intimately.

"I see your point," Vaslav said. "On the visit side of things, I mean."

"She almost succeeded this time. She's already five years into her end stages of the cirrhosis, she can't take another round of slitting her wrists repeatedly through a breakdown," Nanessa added as she reached for the phone that was only an arm's length away on the edge of a desk. "She's not in her twenties, losing control over some man. At her age, with her health, having witnesses won't save her."

Beside him, Vaslav couldn't help but notice how quiet Vera had turned at more of his mother's sordid history and current state—even if it was without all the details. Did that make the woman she had apparently wondered about more human? More *real*?

Did she understand now that every interaction with his mother, even through a third party like her doctor, was like playing with broken glass? Dangerous and delicate. No one left without scars, and he'd been a witness and victim of Natalia's trauma from the time he was born. Hell, oftentimes, she loved to say he was the blame.

Placing the phone, the extra length for cord making it possible, on her lap, the doctor put her hand on the receiver, but hesitated to pick it up. "Maybe she knows that she can't keep doing this, Vaslav, but maybe she doesn't. Either way, it's your call. You can hold the proverbial knife. It might be the last slice, but I'll let you have the say. You've played Russian roulette with my career and personal life for a whole week, and here's where it brings us. Do we have the visit, or not?"

Clearing her throat as delicately as she managed, Vera crossed her arms over her chest with a smug smile that she tipped downward when she told him, "At least I know you kept yourself busy this past week, Vas."

"*Da*—well ..."

He really shouldn't have. The *retirement* said so. Some habits were just damned hard to break.

9.

"*So*," Claire drawled in a teasing manner on the other end of the phone, "how did you like your Christmas gift? I was a big fan of the color, not gonna lie."

In the background of the call, she heard her father say loudly, "But what matters is the size and the fact she can do a triple rollover without even denting the roof, Claire, we've been over this. The color is not the nicest part."

"That's your wrong opinion," Claire replied, "and you're entitled to it, I guess."

Vera's brow puckered in indignation as low chuckles echoed from the end of the bed. She did her best to ignore Vaslav's mostly naked form passing from one corner post of the massive bed to the other. Where she laid directly in the middle of the bed, propped up with several cushions, it wasn't an easy task.

Vaslav made it hard to miss him, really. Instead, she

put her focus on her mother, and the fact that apparently even her parents had knowledge of the custom Hummer that had magically showed up in her driveway on Christmas morning. Everything about the vehicle was made to spec from the leather interior with hand stitched details to the cream-toned paint with just a sheen of pearl for the glossy cherry on top. It wasn't so pink that the color was obvious, but rather, in just the right light one could see the hint of blush in the paint job. It sat sixteen inches off the ground with sparkling white rims and matching steps so she didn't have any trouble at all getting inside. More interesting was the roll bars all around the vehicle.

You know how Russia is with driving—Vaslav's comment when she had pointed out that the cage-like structure of bars might be a little much proved that he clearly didn't think so, and it also wasn't up for debate.

To be fair, his matching Hummer, painted all black—which also showed up at the same time as hers, without the silver ribbon on top like her vehicle had, of course—featured the same roll bars. What was an extra thirty grand on top of the cost of each vehicle, after all? Or that's how Vaslav put it.

"Okay, I won't lie," Vera started to say.

Claire laughed, stopping her from muttering any more. "Just admit it—you loved it."

"I'm not really a *driver*."

"You're just like Demyan. You've gotten too used to people driving you everywhere you need to go. Cabs are not that fun. Dirty, really."

"*Well*—"

"Who is paying that much money for a cab from

Dubna to the city?" Vaslav interjected as he tied a smooth knot around the left bedpost with a navy-blue silk tie.

"Nobody even said anything about money," Vera replied. "Or cabs to the city."

"Yes, but do you know how much that would cost? You visit Hannah too much for that. Spend a few weeks getting comfortable with the Hummer; it's good for these winter roads, too. Besides, I like to drive, *and* be driven. What else are we doing with our time, yeah?"

He even arched a brow to challenge Vera in to denying his statement. She didn't. Other than hiding within the warmth of their home, the two didn't make much time for anything else other than her two- or three-day trips to the city for a night or two with Hannah.

"Well, he makes good points," Claire said, bringing Vera back to the conversation at hand which was more important than the fact Vaslav was now glancing her way with less patience than before. "What else did you get for Christmas?"

Lord, help me, Vera thought.

Vaslav had already finished tying off those ties to the bedposts he'd grabbed from the closet just as her mother was picking up the phone. The deal was simple.

Vera could make the call she promised to her mother, but he wouldn't guarantee how long it would actually last. Maybe she had mentioned something about never being fucked on mink before, and had done so *before* she made that call to her mother.

Time differences were a bitch.

And her husband was insatiable.

Lucky me.

"You didn't hang up on me, did you?" Claire asked.

Vaslav tossed Vera a sinful wink as he turned away from the bed and headed out the open doorway to the sitting room just outside. His figure blackened into a shadow as he walked across the flickering flames crackling in the fireplace.

"Soft and warm things, and some shiny things, too," Vera said, cheekily.

Would her mother figure it out?

Claire, always quick on her feet, quipped, "Let me guess—furs and diamonds."

"It's only a little cliché."

"And you loved every second of it," her mother returned.

Vera didn't have to say a thing.

Yes, she did love it. From the furs and diamonds of every color to the imported fragrances and lush bath products that had been packaged in woven baskets she planned to use to plant in next spring. Spoiled with luxury; adored every moment in between. Who wouldn't bask in that? Her childhood, speckled with memories of when Claire and Demyan were still in the honeymoon stages of their romance and marriage, certainly taught Vera how she wanted to be treated by the man she agreed to love until death parted them.

"He gave me something new every night leading up to tonight," Vera said, not doing well to suppress her giggle at the silliness of it all. "I think he just likes dragging it on."

"As long as he's keeping you busy."

At the remark from Claire, one Vera didn't plan on replying to, Vaslav chose that moment to step back inside the bedroom. Black velvet mink fur hung draped over his right arm while he used his left to close the door between their bedroom and the rest of the master suite. At least, if Mira accidentally thought she was okay to enter the initial space, she knew to absolutely stay out of their bedroom when the door was closed.

"I'll send you pictures of everything tomorrow?" Vera offered.

Claire sighed, already hearing the way her daughter edged them toward ending the call with that question. "You better."

By the time Vera did get her mother off the phone, Vaslav had already thrown her mink coat wide over the end of the bed. He'd waited—as patient as he could while he eyed her like a starving man staring at his last meal—with his hands planted side by side on the curve of the mattress.

Maybe—just maybe, Vera had strung on the phone call a few extra seconds so she could continue to admire the way his tense, expectant position made her feel like prey. The view of his tattooed chest, the colors faded and bleeding over his defined and muscular lines peppered with dark hair, was always a treat for her.

Vera liked being under him best. When he loomed with his substantial size, all rough and heavy against her, she couldn't control herself.

The very second the sleek black phone fell to the bed, signaling the end of her call officially, Vaslav ended any pretenses he had about waiting. His hands found her ankles and yanked hard enough to make her yelp from the bite of his grip.

But his goading grin only had her laughing, breathless with anticipation, when he swung both her legs toward the right bedpost.

"When did I say I was letting you tie me up?" Vera asked.

Not that she tried to kick him away as he worked to secure her leg at the ankle with the silk tie. Just the way he opened her up when he pulled her left leg wide to the other post made her pussy throb with what was to come. Even if she still wore her cotton thong that provided some coverage, she could already feel the slick heat pooling against the fabric as her hips squirmed.

"I like the grey ones best," he said, referring to the color of her underwear. "You see how wet you get right from the start, *biksa*."

"Calling me a slut in Russian just makes it sound better, doesn't it?"

Vaslav's laugh did the dirtiest things to her imagination when he tossed his head back, and his mouth stretched wide. She could practically imagine the way his laugh would feel rumbling against her pussy if he wasn't so far away.

"You're going to make me ruin this coat," she whispered when he shoved his black boxer-briefs down before climbing up onto the bed. If she was wide open and he fucked her the way she knew he would—hard and unforgiving—then they were both going to leave a mess behind. One that her dignity and pride wouldn't allow a dry cleaner to attempt to save.

"Surprise," he murmured, showing his rows of white teeth as he shifted his hands just beyond her shoulders on the bed and loomed over her, "Mira's hiding the second one I had ordered just in case. You're not the only one with a kink for fur."

Vera pouted. "We both know it's morally apprehensible, Vas."

And cruel.

"Who even asked?" he returned just as smug.

Vera reached between them, her hands circling his semi-hard shaft to stroke before he could tell her to do it. A hiss of air split through Vaslav's lips the tighter her fingers became when she came up to the head of his cock. The only part of this man that was soft was the silken skin of his dick, and even that didn't promise not to hurt a little when he fucked her just the way she liked.

That's what made it extra good.

"Get me wet, and use me," he demanded while his hot breath washed down the column of her throat, and he nuzzled at her neck.

She fit his hard cock under the gusset of her thong, and his shaft nestled between her wet folds. Her hand and his weight as he grinded her hips up and down inside her panties kept his cock right where she needed it to be. She was shamefully slick, but it aided the way he glided over the most sensitive parts of her body, and it took no time at all for the ties to be biting into her ankles with every jerky twitch of her legs. It drove her crazy to feel the way Vaslav hardened even more, leaving the marks of his lips and teeth behind on her throat as her moans melted into pants of short breaths.

He slipped inside her as she finally came.

All it took was a shift of his hips, and there he was, every thick inch of him slippery and hard as he filled her. His gentleness dissipated quickly then, while her pussy still clenched tight around his cock from her first orgasm, and he settled in deep.

Half of his weight came down on her. One of his hands helped to keep her pinned to the bed while his teeth found her jaw. She whined from the sharp nip of his teeth as his fingers wove with hers and he shoved their connected fists into the bed.

The sting from his bite was only soothed by the suckle of his lips and tease of his tongue over the same spot before he murmured, "Tell me what you want me to do."

He held her tight to him.

Still so deep, too.

It was so easy to tell him what she liked because he did it all so fucking well, and enjoyed pulling every orgasm he could from her body while he did it. It pleased him, and that only turned her on more. She wasn't ashamed to feel like a greedy slut who couldn't get enough of a man; she was exactly that for Vas, and it didn't bother her a bit.

"*What*, my *kisska*?" Vaslav asked, hoarse with his own anticipation. He did well to hold back from just going in on her the way he wanted to. Sometimes he did, and no matter what, he rode her hard, let her sleep well, and loved her softly in the mornings.

If they were good mornings for him, that was. Good meaning his migraines were gone, if not minor, or he wasn't stuck in the bathroom on his knees.

If not, every step she took throughout the day, and the twinges that followed from where he held her too hard or otherwise, served their purpose to mark the man's territory until he was back again. Her body was his—to use, please, or tease. She wore every tiny bruise and lovebite like she was the canvas, and those marks were his art.

Choke me, fuck me … hurt me, she wanted to say, but

every racing desire she let slip through her mind didn't quite feel like enough.

"Love me," she told him before his lips came down on hers for a fervent kiss.

God knew he would.

Vera only had one thought left for Vaslav to bleed away with the rest of her rationale and self-control: *Happy New Year to me.*

*

The rap of knuckles against the dining room table drew Vera's head up from the pages of her latest book. As it turned out, Mira was also a big reader and had amassed quite a selection of novels in her set of suites on the third floor. While she had already filled her available shelves with books, the rest piled up on stands and in corners, all with cracked spines and dog-eared pages.

Vera's favorite kind of book.

A well-loved one.

"I found something I thought you might like to see," Mira said where she stood in the alcove between the dining room and kitchen. In her hands, she held up what appeared to be an old photo album.

"What's that?" Vera asked.

Mira shrugged. "Vaslav's mother—well, years ago, I worked for her. She wasn't a particularly sentimental woman, and wasn't one to display her memories and trinkets. Once when I had some extra time, I put this together for her but ..."

Trailing off, Mira lifted her shoulders again as if that was explanation enough to clear up why she had the album and not the woman it was meant for.

"She also isn't one for gifts that don't come with a price tag attached," Mira added with a roll of her eyes. "If you get what I mean."

Ah.

Yeah, Vera did.

"Could I see?" she asked.

Mira smiled. "Of course, that's why I got it out. Well, I thought of it after you had asked last week if there were any other pictures of Vaslav's mother other than the very young ones in the main entry."

Those toddler-aged black and white glamor shots of a white-haired tot weren't exactly what Vera had been looking for, either. Nonetheless, Mira promised to look for more, and so she had. Having no one else except for Vaslav to talk about his mother—which he wasn't keen on doing—Vera took a chance on Mira.

And struck gold.

A woman who had not only worked under Natalia Pashkova as a caretaker for years, she also considered herself a friend of the woman once.

But you have to understand, Mira had said when she told Vera that fact, *you only really think you're her friend for as long as she needs you.*

Even though the book she'd been reading was just starting to get to the best part, Vera flipped it shut and shoved it across the table to make room for the large, leatherbound album Mira placed in front of her. Only an initial was embossed on the front.

A cursive N.

"It's not chronological or anything," Mira explained as Vera flipped open the sturdy cover to find the first thing memorialized between sheets of plastic was a newspaper article.

Socialite Natalia Pashkova Marries Sixth Husband.

Vera's brow jumped high at the political name attached to the headline. A man with significant power in the Federation.

"That barely lasted six months," Mira noted. "One of her longest, and not her last."

Huh.

"She was mid-forties there?" Vera asked, pointing to the age the article wrote attached to a grainy image of a thin, willowy woman draped in white silk and hanging off the arm of a man turning away from the camera. Her husband, Vera thought, but she couldn't be sure.

Mira nodded. "Hmm, oh, yes. In the right light, if she's not been binge drinking for days then she barely looked a day over thirty right up until these last few years. Age caught up quick."

Vera considered all the different things she knew about Vaslav's history with his mother just by the comments he made. It prompted her to ask, "How much of that was thanks to his money paying for her youth?"

A smack of Mira's lips echoed in the room.

Vera hummed knowingly to herself. *Yep.*

Like she thought.

"Anyway," Mira said, pointing to the album as she backed away from the table at the sound of Marrow's echoing bark from the rear of the house. "You're welcome to look through it. I showed Vaslav once, but ... well, you know how he is."

Oh, Vera could only imagine.

Mira went searching for the cause of Marrow's bark that continued without a break between each sharp woof. In the rear of the house with Vaslav's den and enclosed porch, the dog had all the warmth, scraps, and stuffy toys to destroy that he needed. He only left the house for a total of an hour or two a day, depending on the temperature, and the dog even held his faculties for a full day if he truly only wanted to go out once. Between her husband, and Mira, Vera didn't have to do very much for Marrow or handle him. He didn't go further into the house than the back hallway leading to Vaslav's den in the rear, and they'd only had one run in late at night when the dog melted into the shadows.

She really hadn't known that Vaslav left the door open between the den and the porch for the dog, and he forgot to mention it when he asked her to grab the day planner he kept on his desk as a running to-do list and reminder of other important tasks.

Sometimes, he used it as a journal, too.

Her suggestion.

Everyone needed a place to get out their thoughts, after all.

"Marrow, *stop!*" Mira yelled into the hallway as Vera had just started to flip through the next pages of the album. Finally, she had a picture—several, actually— to put a face and more details on the life and story of a stranger Vera wasn't entirely sure that she wanted to know.

Even if she had asked Vaslav not to have the visit with his mother; at the time, proclaiming it to be for her own cowardice because of what she'd done. Maybe she was just immature enough for Vaslav to believe it, but had she said it was to benefit the woman's mental health, she didn't think he would have cared.

In fact, she knew he wouldn't.

The woman was dying, anyway.

Slowly.

The cirrhosis would do it eventually as her son had no intention of paying for a liver transplant in another country for a long-term alcoholic that had abused and tortured him for years while piddling away his wealth. It wouldn't matter, as that probably wouldn't help or succeed in the end. It was what it was—Vaslav's exact words to Vera on the day they stepped out of the Roseville facility.

So be it.

His mother's sordid history didn't need to be entirely dug up by Vera simply because she had nothing else better to do with her time, apparently.

"Vera, are you having a guest?" Mira asked.

The question had her slamming the album shut and leaving it behind at the table as she heard Mira encouraging Marrow to enter back into the den where she could shut him behind the safety of a door. Despite knowing what the dog had done to Igor's hand, and anyone else who took his wrath, Mira wasn't scared of Marrow.

"No," Vera said, heading for the front door at the sound of wheels crunching over icy gravel. Anyone in the upstairs master suites would have a good view of the vehicle and occupants parked at the front of the house. "But only five of us have keys to the gate, so."

Vaslav, Vera, Mira, Igor, and ...

"What is *Hannah* doing here?" Vaslav asked, his voice a booming echo from the upstairs where he had spent the better part of his day. Shades drawn, no fire to keep the rooms chilled, and entirely alone. It made Vera lonelier than ever, but when he wanted her, she always went. As little time as that usually was—she took it, and only helped him.

"Tell her if she's using cabs again, she walks from the gate, Vera," Vaslav shouted down the massive stairwell.

"Stop it, she's not walking from the gate in January, Vaslav," Vera called back. "Don't be ridiculous."

A door slammed in response.

Frankly, he shouldn't have allowed Vera the choice in her extra gate key.

"Could you put that album away for me to look through later?" Vera asked Mira once the woman was satisfied with Marrow's confinement and had crossed the foyer.

"Of course. Ask Hannah if she's staying for dinner, yes?"

"Sure."

While Vera couldn't see her friend through the frosty glass of the windows next to the door, she still opened it with a smile, expecting Hannah to be close enough to hug. *Almost*. The cab was just pulling away while Hannah climbed the bottom steps.

"I'm not walking from there in this cold," she said, already referring to the gate.

Vera didn't mind the chill. "I'll take a walk and lock it later."

Slung over her shoulder, Hannah carried a weekender bag. In her hand, she held tight to a plain, white plastic grocery bag that Vera couldn't quite see through to make out the box-shaped impressions bulging out the sides.

"Are you staying the night?" Vera asked.

"I bribed a certain someone to come get me tomorrow, so if you don't mind, yeah, I'm gonna stay."

Assuming her friend meant Igor, Vera only

shrugged. She didn't mind at all.

Vera moved back like Hannah might come right inside, but her friend waved her further out on the stoop once she was under the entrance alcove.

"Shut the door a bit," Hannah said, shifting the bag so she had each looped handle ready to open in both hands.

"What is wrong with you? It's freezing, let's go into the house," Vera said, but Hannah didn't move. "Why didn't you call?"

"Look," her friend demanded.

Then, she opened up the bag.

One glimpse down told Vera all she needed to know. Every pink and white rectangular box couldn't be mistaken with their big plus and negative symbols right on the front. She damned near had a flashback of her foolish teenage years when she really hadn't known how biology, and her own body, worked, and the anxiety she felt picking up her first pregnancy test at the store. She couldn't look at those boxes for one more second without wanting to scream.

Vera's head snapped back up, and Hannah's eyes were already terrifyingly wide. No woman bought a half of a dozen pregnancy tests because she wasn't pregnant. In denial, definitely, but little else.

"Holy shit," she muttered.

Hannah nodded, face whitening with every bob of her head. "Yeah, Vera. Holy fucking shit. You'll sit with me, right? Like, after I take them or whatever?"

"You don't even have to ask."

10.

"My God," Vaslav groaned, "won't you just go to bed?"

"No."

The soft response was still short and curt enough to tell Vaslav that Vera was getting annoyed that he kept asking. To be fair, that was only his third time in fifteen minutes. That didn't mean he thought she *shouldn't* take her pretty, sweet ass straight to bed where she could actually get some rest. She had better things to do than what she was—straddling his mostly naked, sweaty form on their bathroom's floor while she massaged his head with those dainty fingers of hers at three in the morning.

Her friend slept down the hall.

For the *second* night.

Mostly because Vaslav had unfortunately learned earlier in the day that the person who would be running to pick Hannah up was someone he couldn't have within one hundred kilometers of his home.

Kiril.

All done with innocent intentions, according to the two involved in the plan, but he had still put a stop to that shit the second he knew it existed. He could do without any trouble that might be following Kiril at the moment.

So, no. Not happening.

Or so he thought.

Because the woman on top of him had different things to say, and he hated when she made more sense than his irrational instincts that sometimes steered him wrong. He didn't have so much pride that he couldn't admit it.

"You know Kiril was the one who had the connection to the man supplying your ounce a week, right?" Vera asked, breaking the silence in the bathroom once more.

He despised suffering, but worse, he hated the pity he felt for himself when he was in the throes of the worst of his migraines. Pity was worse because it did even less than his pain did for him at the end of the day; utterly useless, but almost always present.

"Igor doesn't have the time," Vera added. "He barely makes it out here once a week—and why do you think he was coming out here, anyway?"

Right.

Kiril. The connection. The ounce of *premium*, medical grade THC that Vaslav was smoking a week. At this point, he needed to move to concentrates or elsewise to make it easier on his goddamn lungs. He hadn't smoked like that in years, and while the smoke had taken some getting used to, it barely caused a dull throb now.

The benefits far outweighed the cons, in his

opinion, when it was an ounce of weed a week or a handful of Demerol a day. He could only play that game with his fucking pain for so long, frankly. And the last time he had to dry out off the pills, even if it was while he'd been hitting the bottle too heavily, was enough to tell Vaslav—well, to hell with his lungs. His risk for seizure and death was higher than ever if he had to go that route again.

Another reason he hated having a doctor at his beck and call. Bogdan, when in a pleasant mood, was actually a good conversationalist. He also had a formally frank way of delivering Vaslav's eventual outcome, and how that death would occur, whenever he stepped out of line.

He should call the man less often.

Who knew he was such a sucker for punishment?

"You're not even listening to me, are you?" Vera asked.

Worse, her hands left his head altogether even if his scalp could still feel the way those last rakes of her fingernails had glided over sweaty skin.

"No, only a little," he admitted.

Vera grumped a sigh, flattening her arms over her chest.

Vaslav really needed to follow along with Vera's conversation if he was going to give her a valid reason to drop all of the nonsense. Even if that meant laying his overheated, overly sensitive body on a cold tiled floor while his wife—who really should be sleeping— eased his pain by barely a notch with her tired hands.

He knew they were tired.

The lack of give and flex in her fingers before she'd stopped, probably stiff by now as the two of them had been at this for a good hour, was proof even if she didn't complain. The most selfish creature he'd ever known was himself, and yet, the guilt gnawed at him with every sleepless night he dragged out of this beautiful, vibrant woman.

"I *was* listening," Vaslav corrected as he squinted through the slits in his eyelids to eye his quietly contemplating wife. "I stopped, no?"

A disapproving tilt of her head answered him back.

Vaslav tried not to let it eat away at his heart too much. Goddammit. Why did she have to be the one who made him feel human?

"Not on purpose," he added after another few seconds of silence.

It wasn't a lie, and he wouldn't have said it otherwise. Locked in pain left him trapped in his mind and thoughts; Vera knew those troubles of his all too well.

Her anger softened only slightly above him. He let out a small breath, and closed his eyes to avoid the strain of seeking out her face in the dimly lit space.

"Let me paint you a picture," Vaslav started, still keeping his eyes shut.

Vera snorted. "Another one of these, huh?"

"Stop it, there's only one time I enjoy the sound of your whining."

He heard the pop when her jaw snapped close.

"Rude," Vera muttered shortly after.

And yet, not untrue.

"The picture," Vaslav continued, one of his hands lifting from the floor and waving a circle like he was making an invisible frame before he dropped his arm back down to the tiles with a slap. "Let's go back to that, yeah? The kid is being watched by certain people to see if he's usable for them. He's also a runner for

Igor—doing whatever, whenever. I have to be a silent, uninvolved observer or skin is in the game."

"What about the picture?" Vera asked.

At another time, he'd truly enjoy her sarcasm. This wasn't one of those.

"The point is that I'm not fucking in it," Vaslav snapped, scowling. "Isn't that obvious?"

Vera gave no warning before her weight lifted from Vaslav's body, and he opened his eyes wide enough just in time to see her heading for the bathroom's door.

"Where are you going?"

"To bed," Vera replied without a pause to her steps. "I'll call the car service we used when my parents were in the city—I'm sure they'll have something. You're right, I need to learn to drive."

Vaslav didn't move from the floor to stop Vera from leaving other than the slight lift of his hand that reached for her, even if only in a silent demand to wait. Frankly, he didn't have the strength for more, and it was going to take him a moment to get up, if he really needed to.

"Vera—"

At the door, she turned to look back at him, shrugging. "It's fine. You rationalize something as ridiculous as Kiril driving from the city to here, but have no issues with me making the drives. Alone, by the way. Like somehow saying you're retired, changing a tattoo, and a few rumors change anything about who you are or the things you've done."

That made him squint.

"What do you know about the things I've done, *kisska*?"

It was a genuine question.

For a few reasons …

Vera took the bait, but not the way he expected her to. "Enough to say you know there's a reason why you don't want any skin in the game. Your words, not mine."

Fair.

Reasonable, even.

"The problem you miss—or overlook, rather," he corrected with an indifferent roll of his shoulders against the floor while his gaze fixated on the vaulted ceiling overhead, "is that it wouldn't make a difference, my love." His head fell back to the side, and his gaze landed on her as he smiled sadly.

He could finally finish painting that earlier picture for her even if it would shatter what remained of her rose-colored glasses regarding their marriage and life together. Hell, he thought she had already figured it out by now.

Shame.

"What's done has already been done—I wrote the past. Nothing, not even me, gets to determine the future that's yet to be made because of it. You see? Either the process and the oath means something to men who someday might want to find themselves in my position"— *retired; a thief out of the game*—"or it doesn't. And either my past and legacy is enough of a warning to make it valuable and important for those men to leave me alone, or it isn't. But what's done is done, all the bodyguards in the world won't make a difference."

"Are we just sitting ducks?" Vera asked.

"Try not to think of it that way," he returned easily, the joking tone belying the pain stabbing into the base of his skull, "who does that help, yeah?"

"Vaslav—"

"They'd have to get us together," he interjected before his wife could concern herself over minor details of a plot that they didn't even know was afoot. This was why he didn't like to share his thought process regarding certain things. While he planned for events that may never happen because it was what managed his more obsessive tendencies, others simply worked themselves into a panicked mess.

Good for nothing.

"Which we'll rarely ever be, and certainly not with enough forethought to let anyone else have the knowledge except in this house and on this property," he added the impossibility under his breath.

Not quiet enough, apparently.

"So, what, just one of us gets killed or—"

"If it's me, then it was never meant for you," Vaslav explained.

"And if it's me?"

Well …

"God save them all," he said.

"I don't even know what to say to that."

"I didn't realize we had that chat for you to respond, honestly." Vaslav sighed, scrubbing a hand over his mouth and down his throat before finally shoving himself higher into a sitting position. It did nothing for the current weakness in his stomach. A few deep gulps of air helped with the swaying of his shoulders, but little else. "Christ," he mumbled into his hand. "You've got to put that other shit out of your mind—we won't live scared. What good does that do?"

If she believed him, Vera didn't say.

"Come to bed," Vera urged instead. "I'll help you

to sleep."

Or something close to it.

She always did, that was a certainty he could count on when it really counted. At the moment, a couple of blissful hours of near-sleep with her was a promise he couldn't refuse. His body ached for her softness back, and the clean sheets that she'd put on their bed earlier in the day teased him from where he sat on the cold, hard floor.

"I know it doesn't always make sense," Vaslav said, groaning when he stumbled his way to his feet. His wife, still standing with her arms crossed over her chest in the doorway, remained like a silent statue as she waited for him. Stripped down to nothing but a blue sports bra and matching boyshort panties, she was his every wet dream come true. Wrapped around his finger, happy to be under his thumb, and wickedly willing to follow him anywhere or do anything he asked of her. Yes, she was perfect.

Except he couldn't even get his dick to react in that moment. Not even a pathetic twitch to say the monster was alive to notice.

Jesus.

Fuck his moods.

The pain.

All of it.

She stayed still until he was next to her in the doorway. Tipping her chin up so that there was no mistaking the way she looked him in the eye, Vera asked, "What difference does it make—a trip made to Dubna once a week for Igor, or Kiril? Which looks like you're sticking your hand in the pot that isn't yours anymore, Vas?"

There she went again.

Making sense.

He'd deal with that, and what he wanted to do about it, tomorrow. That was the best he could do considering his current circumstances.

"I need to lay down," Vaslav mumbled.

Noticing the unsteadiness he suddenly found standing on two feet, Vera was quick to tangle her arms inside his. Before long, his back found the safe comfort of their bed, and by the time he rolled over onto his side, already lost in the pressure building inside his head, fireworks of pain lighting up behind his clenched eyelids, Vera was on her side of the bed.

Cloaked in darkness, because he couldn't bear to open his eyes again, Vaslav settled into the gentle strokes of Vera's tired hands. Her lips pressed to his forehead with a kiss, and a soft breath that somehow felt cooler in temperature than the rest of his body.

"I'm here," she assured him.

Even if he hadn't asked or said a thing. That was the most beautiful part about her. He wouldn't keep doing this—living like this—if he didn't have her.

11.

"*Pup*," Vaslav greeted from the top of the stairs.

At the very bottom where Kiril waited, rocking on two feet standing ahead of the passenger side of his sleek, black coupe—compliments of Vaslav's bank account the previous year—the boy grinned back. He didn't seem at all bothered by the deep scowl set into Vaslav's face at the very sight of him, nor was he concerned with the way he continued to scan behind Kiril, further down the hill and driveway.

For what?

Anything.

Rocking back on his heels, and stuffing his hands deep into the pockets of his parka with the fur-trimmed hood, Kiril replied, "Hey, boss."

Goddammit, kid.

"I'm not the boss," Vaslav told him.

And if he had to correct Kiril too many times on that topic, one of them wouldn't be happy. The other one would only hurt.

Kiril shrugged like it didn't make a difference to him either way, and that stupid, silly grin on his face didn't leave, either. "So, you had a chat with Igor this morning, then?"

Obviously.

The kid wouldn't be there otherwise. The final words of his conversation with Vera the night before had certainly left an impact on his mind when morning came, and he couldn't stop thinking about it. Igor hadn't appreciated the early morning call to chat.

It was what it was.

"How's the legal shit?" Vaslav asked instead of discussing his conversation with Igor. "A proper fuckin' mess, the last I heard, yeah?"

"Better," Kiril deadpanned.

"How so?"

"I don't sleep in the same bed twice, and the cops don't pick me up on the streets everyday for a game of Twenty Questions because they can't keep track of me, and I just think the fuckers like messing with me 'cause they've been on a first name basis with me since I was eleven. But who's to say, you know? Otherwise, it's fine," Kiril explained with a delivery that said he couldn't care less about the topic, and that was something Vaslav could not relate to in the slightest. "At least, Igor's not all in my business when I'm sleeping with somebody new every night. Half the time, he doesn't know where I am, either. It's working."

That quip lifted Vaslav's brows high.

"Oh, to be that young and stupid again," Vaslav murmured.

Kiril seemed okay with it, though.

"You'll make the weekly trips from here on out,"

Vaslav explained. "Todays the only day you're not waiting at the gate for someone to come down and meet you—do you hear me?"

A crinkle turned Kiril's nose upward. "Is the weed good, at least?"

Out of all the things the teenager could ask or say, that was the point he wanted to get clarified. Vaslav sighed heavily, his wary gaze never leaving Kiril as he ran through the many ways he wanted to teach the kid how to mind and behave.

But honestly?

None of it would do Kiril any good. Full of youth, still wild, and currently free. Undoubtedly, he made good money running for Igor and handling his tasks. Which probably fed into his late-night lifestyle and whatever else he did to keep himself distracted from being bored. See, that's when kids like Kiril, not entirely grown but parentless nonetheless, thought too much. About their past and pains. *Everything.*

At the moment, Vaslav bet Kiril was living the dream. The whole world sat in his hands, and he could do anything with it ... if he wanted. What he did, however, was another matter.

"You tell me," Vaslav settled on saying in regards to the quality of the cannabis. "You're the one with the connection, pup."

Kiril smirked, and pulled both hands from his parka's pockets to produce what had been hiding in the left side. "Yeah, the weed's good."

The tightly rolled bag of weed looked just the same as every previous package Igor had dropped off after making the trip to Dubna. Right down to the red sticker strip that wrapped the middle of the roll to keep the cannabis nice and fresh.

Kiril started up the steps with the package in his hand already outstretched to Vaslav who didn't plan to move from where he stood under the safety of the alcove. Not while the wind was blustery and colder than a polar bear's asshole, anyway. He snatched the baggie from a laughing Kiril once the kid was close enough to do so, and then Vaslav pointed back down at the running car with exhaust fumes clinging to the air.

"You better have good winter tires on that damn thing," he told Kiril.

Over his shoulder, the boy waved a hand, indifferent. "Yeah, yeah. All studded."

Vaslav sighed harder than ever.

He shouldn't *care*.

His biggest irritation with Kiril was that he did—so much so that he wondered how much the kid would make of his life and future if Vaslav just sat him down and spilled what he knew about being a young man like Kiril with the world at his fingertips, and danger luring him in. For some reason, his urge to spill those secrets, some that had shaped him more than others, with a kid that Vaslav knew still had a lot of learning and growing yet to do before it would make a real difference, irked him. He wasn't used to people who were easy to like.

"Hannah will be out shortly," Vaslav said, heading for the warmth waiting for him behind the front door. "She was just packing up as I let her know you were coming up the drive."

"You were watching for me?"

Vaslav's shoulders tensed, but he didn't turn around to face Kiril when he muttered, "I watch for everybody."

The kid wasn't special in that regard.

Vaslav yanked open the door, willing to let those be his parting words for Kiril. The frustratingly cocky fool had plans of his own to say goodbye, apparently, quipping, "See ya next week, boss."

Vaslav let the door slam shut at that comment. He didn't ease up on the fucking swing when it closed just to make the point on how he felt crystal clear. He needed to pretend like he didn't hear Kiril's muffled laughter on the other side of the door.

Fucking kid.

Frankly, he had better things to do, which included soon having his wife alone. Once her little friend went home. After he rolled a blunt as thick as his thumb and smoked until he was numb, his day and evening could only go up from there.

At the back of the house, Marrow's constant, sharp bark, alerting to their guest he had yet to see because he was stuck in the rear porch attached to the den yet again, quieted at Vaslav's booming shout.

"Hannah! Your ride's here!"

*

Vaslav's plans to spend the rest of his day and evening didn't quite go as he intended. His own fault, really. He'd left the small tray he used to keep his cannabis supplies all in one spot in his den, and decided to roll the blunt downstairs instead of carrying the whole kit up to the bathroom and risking spilling it if he had a fucking episode.

He never could predict when that was about to happen, but it always signaled the same thing—the worst parts of what would be a raging migraine wasn't far behind.

Nonetheless, after rolling what he considered to be a satisfactory blunt with a vanilla flavored cigarillo, Vaslav found the bathroom with the best exhaust fan in the house had already been put to use. Technically.

Mira barely glanced over her shoulder at him as she sat her plastic carton of supplies she liked to clean on the counter next to the sink when he walked into the room. The lighter in one hand, and blunt hanging out of his mouth told the story of his intentions without him needing to say anything, but the cock of Mira's left eyebrow said a lot, too.

It wasn't often that she made her way into their private spaces to clean—Vera did most of that, including stripping their sheets regularly, and scrubbing down their bathroom. Her tidy nature wouldn't let her sit still, and if she wanted to claim all but a few rooms in the very large home to clean, so be it.

It was hers now, after all.

Mira understood, it seemed, but she still made her rounds once or twice a week to change out towels, add to whatever they might need, or otherwise. Vaslav wasn't long swinging around to head out of the bathroom at the sight of Mira doing her work. Better if he didn't bother her, honestly. Besides, she had a time every night—one she stuck to—where she liked to head to her rooms upstairs, and be alone.

Given how much she did for him, Vaslav tried not to interfere in Mira's personal time more than he usually did.

The half-bath down the hall attached to the guest bedroom was a poor second choice for a good room with decent ventilation in the house, but Vaslav had no interest in going back downstairs to smoke outside. That was his last resort in the middle of winter.

He loved the weed; it *helped*. It also had its short list of cons that he easily managed.

Including the smell. He didn't like that. Not when it stuck to everything, lingering and clinging to fabrics, surfaces, and everything in between. A hot shower after a blunt was his new favorite hobby, and he planned to get Vera to join him for exactly that once he was done doing his business.

Mira should be finished cleaning by then, and his wife would certainly be done with her goodbyes. He couldn't see Kiril standing out in the cold for any longer than he had to while Hannah and Vera dragged their departure on, although he wouldn't put it past his wife to catch up with Kiril, either, considering how long it had been since the two last saw one another.

Vaslav had lots of time to smoke—he didn't rush it, never did. Every inhale, once he'd lit the blunt while he used the closed commode as a stool, came in slow, and he held it deep before releasing the thick, dank cloud of grey heaven up to the ceiling where the fan waited to weakly suck it away. He'd have the small space hotboxed in no time at all. His chest burned with the exertion of his lungs to hold in the heady smoke—he did have a personal best, but he would keep that secret to himself—until his throat choked to let it out.

He despised the smoke, but given he'd been out of anything to use to settle his nerves, ease his stomach, and help his sleep—the cannabis did it all—for over a day, Vaslav was due. He made no apologies for the fact that he would suffer later when the head high wore off, and he was left with the lingering smell of smoking in a bathroom that he shouldn't have used.

Shit.

He hadn't even covered the crack in the door.

Distracted, and *pleased*, with his current state, Vaslav didn't realize how long the ash on the end of his blunt had become until his hand cut through the air a little too fast, and the tip fell. The bit of cherry red coal in the ash hit his pants, and he swatted it away to the floor.

Making a bigger mess. Just his luck.

While his wife didn't mind his new vice to manage his pain and lack of sleep—mostly because she was all too happy to partake with him—the other lady in the house couldn't say the same. Mira, that was.

She hated everything about cannabis from the smell to the time it took Vaslav to finish a blunt. Not that she complained too much, but it was enough for Vaslav to at least consider Mira's feelings.

The quickly diminishing coals wouldn't do any damage to the tiled floor, but he still reached for the clean pile of washcloths that should be waiting in the basket behind the toilet. A damp one would wipe the ashes up easily, but he found the basket was empty. Not unusual as Hannah had been using the space during her stay, and Mira probably hadn't gotten to it yet to clean and replace what was needed.

He went looking for the next best thing—paper towel—or whatever was under the sink's closed cabinets. All he discovered there was a white plastic bag stuffed next to a pile of towels.

Vaslav shouldn't have opened the bag.

It ruined his whole fucking day.

12.

"*Vera!*"

It took Vera no time at all in their new marriage to become accustomed to random shouts of her name from another part of the house. So, even the second time Vaslav yelled her name from down the hall outside the master suites, she didn't even glance up from the leatherbound album in her hands.

She had no reason to rush and put it down. If what Vaslav wanted was her, then he would make his way to where she was one way or another.

While flipping to the next page in the album full of memories, Vera called back to her husband, "I'm in our room, Vas!"

She could have added for him to relax considering how fast his footsteps pounded down the hall, but she opted to keep her mouth shut. Besides, the photo album was more than enough to hold her attention while Vaslav pitched a fit about whatever.

Mira had managed to keep quite a few photographs

of and newspaper clippings about Natalia Pashkova over the years. The album was almost entirely full. A lot were from when the woman was a young girl with the later, adult years focusing more on what Mira had been able to cut out of the papers.

One, near the middle of the album, was one Vera considered asking for. Not a clipping from a newspaper, the photograph that had been folded in the middle one too many times had also been scribbled on in the corner.

With a date and names.

Vaslav, and his mother.

She looked barely older than mid-teens—*maybe*—and the newborn, swaddled in white in the grayscale image, didn't look to be happy with the way his teenage mother held him as he openly squalled. Of course, Natalia smiled for the photo.

Not *nicely*.

Forced, mostly.

And the way her arm clung to the swaddled infant, almost like she'd rather not be doing it at all, cut at Vera's heart in a way she couldn't explain. Which was why Vera had the strangest urge to rip the image out of the album and destroy it.

No wonder Vaslav hated his mother—from the start, it looked like she hadn't even wanted him, as if even holding him was more than she could stand to do. Who needed a physical reminder of that kind of pain?

"What is this?" Vaslav demanded from behind Vera.

She closed the photo album with a snap, although he simply opted to ignore it for the most part, and turned on the cushion where she sat next to the fireplace to face Vaslav in the entry to their suites. Only giving him part of her attention as she reached over to put the photo album on the coffee table, she couldn't see what he held in his hand as he approached the back of the chesterfield.

"I asked you a question," he said.

The tone did it for her.

Nasty and mean.

He had *all* of her attention now. Whether he wanted it or not.

"What is your problem?" Vera asked, simply turning around on the cushion instead of standing like he might want her to. "Hannah's gone, Mira's making something to eat, and even the dog is outside now."

Each of those things were something he had either taken offense to over the past couple of days, or found a reason to bitch about when he was in a mood, and not coping well. She didn't see where his issue remained when he currently had every reason to be pleased.

All things considered.

Vera sniffed the air, and smirked at the familiar smell she found lingering there. Skunky and unmistakable, with or without the bloodshot eyes of her husband trying to stare her down, she knew damn well what that smell meant by now. No doubt, the weed was also the reason for his quick disappearance while she said her goodbyes to Hannah downstairs. "You smell like you had a good time down the hall—"

Vaslav wasn't impressed. He didn't even blink an eye at her comment. "Vera, what in the hell is this?"

The second time he asked that question, it came out a lot more forceful—but also panicked—than the first. He also lifted his arm high enough for her to see what the chesterfield had been keeping hidden, and the sight of the white plastic thrusting toward her in mid-air sucked the breath from her lungs.

All at once, everything made sense. From his reaction to the overreaction. Maybe she hadn't explained Hannah's reason for showing up out of the blue, but to be fair, her friend practically begged Vera to keep it a secret for the time being.

For a few reasons.

Not all were good.

Nonetheless, she intended to keep that promise to Hannah. Unless it caused a bigger issue, and clearly it had.

"Vas," she tried to say.

He wouldn't give her a chance to, though. He gave her no time to speak.

"*Net*—what the fuck is this?" His gaze narrowed on her with every word he spat, but she refused to shrink under the weight of it. "Get to the bathroom. *Now*."

Vera blinked, but didn't move. "Excuse me?"

"Did I stutter?" Vaslav rounded the arm of the chesterfield before Vera had a chance to reply, let alone think of one, and in the next second, he yanked her up from the floor with a rough grip that had her stumbling over the cushion left behind. He shoved her ahead of him, toward the doorway of their bedroom and the master's en suite bathroom with a muttered, "Get going, right now."

"Stop it, Vaslav—*let me talk*!"

Vera swung around on him fast—her hands up and ready to shove him back if need be—but his body acted like a brick wall. No one, and certainly not her, would be getting though him anytime soon. Right there in the threshold of their bedroom, he blocked her in and made it clear by the way his hands flattened to either side of the doorjamb that he would not be moving. All the while, he said nothing, but he didn't have to when his actions spoke loud enough for the both of them. Like an animal backed into a corner with no escape, all she could do was stare up at him, horrified that he would treat her in such a way.

Her desire to talk was practically nil.

"*Move*," she told him.

Vaslav teeth grinded, his jaw sliding back and forth each time, but his gaze didn't break away from hers. What she found there *stung*. The way he could make a person feel so insignificant under his pensive stare couldn't be matched.

The man was a pro.

"I will move," he told her, that tense jaw of his still working over that anger like gnawing down the enamel on his teeth would make it all go away, "when you piss on one of those fuckin' sticks."

At that, Vera took a step back.

"I'm not pregnant," she said honestly.

Vaslav jerked his chin upward at her, muttering right back, "Yeah, and I'll know it when I see it. Go take a test."

Her genuineness meant nothing. It sure didn't help their current situation, or the bull of a man blocking her exit from the bedroom. She was slightly less concerned about that part of what was happening at the moment, but only because something wasn't right.

Vaslav could be a prick.

An asshole on his *good* days.

Blunt honesty was his best friend, and even better

when it hurt. The truth usually did, anyways, according to him.

What he never did was manhandle Vera. Not outside of their intimacy; he rarely did more than raise his voice. Oh, they had snippy moments. When she could rile him up enough for a proper argument, those were some of the best conversations the two had ever had together. She loved him best when he was grumpy and willing to hold a conversation that included more than grunts for replies.

She loved him all the time in between, too.

He didn't *shove* her, though—never just made her do things, whether that meant bringing him tea or moving her across the fucking room. This wasn't like Vaslav.

Not with her.

Something was wrong. It had to be more than just him discovering pregnancy tests if this was how he treated her because of it.

Vaslav pointed at the light streaming into the dimly lit bedroom—as usual, he'd pulled all the curtains to keep the space cloaked in chilly darkness—from the connecting bathroom. "I'm not going to tell you to do it again."

Vera could have said a lot of things in response to that thinly veiled threat. She should have, definitely. Instead, she decided to draw an invisible line in between herself and her husband, and then she gave him the option to cross it with her next question

"Or what?" she asked. "Are you going to make me take a pregnancy test for you? Will you stand there and hold it for me, too, Vas?"

His sneer came off cold when he replied, "Is that what'd you like to do? We can—*da*? You're barely a hundred and thirty-five pounds when you're soaking wet."

The last words hissed out of his mouth.

Vera stood a little straighter.

"Get real. You're being ridiculous."

Maybe she slung that insult at him one too many times, and it did nothing for him anymore to snap Vaslav out of his behavior. He loosened his stance in the doorway, and even folded his arms over his chest while he stared her down. His eyebrow cocked with a silent challenge she heard well while the plastic bag with what remained of Hannah's unused pregnancy tests swung in his grip.

Try me—his posture screamed it.

Vera had enough.

"Give me them," she said, reaching for the bag.

Silently, Vaslav handed the handle loops over. She wasn't particularly polite about the way she snatched the bag from his hand, and she didn't soften the sarcasm when she told him, "I'm so glad Hannah only used four so I have two left to placate you."

Vaslav's expression didn't change. "What about Hannah?"

Vera dead-stared her husband as she backed away from him while pulling one of the two tests remaining in the bag out. It didn't matter now—he wanted her to take a fucking test so badly that he would be willing to force her to do so, then she'd take a test for him.

"No big deal," she told Vaslav, waving the pink and white pregnancy test box for him to see even though the man couldn't take his eyes off of it. Like it might bite him or something. "It's just a piece of plastic. That's useless to me, by the way, since I'm not the one who's pregnant. Good thing you didn't open the trash can down the hall, you would have found the used ones from yesterday."

That time, Vaslav's brows lifted subtly. He remained silent, though, observing her head into the bathroom from where he had stayed in the doorway between the connecting suites. Once Vera had made it to the commode and shoved her leggings and panties down to her knees, Vaslav had come to stand just beyond the bathroom door. She discarded the packaging for the test, but hesitated before doing anything further.

Instead, she sat down on the lid of the toilet seat, flicking that strip of thin plastic against her palm. Vaslav couldn't look away from the pregnancy test, not even to see the way tears threatened to spill from his wife's eyes.

It wasn't right.

None of this.

"I'll take the test for you," Vera said, "but you have to tell me why you want me to."

Vaslav's chin tipped up an inch, and he sucked air through his teeth like he might actually be considering her request as if it was a valid offer. "I didn't realize my demand came with an opportunity for a counteroffer."

"Vaslav, I took a pregnancy test a month ago before I got my Depo shot. Standard. I get one every time. It was negative."

Vera didn't care about the pregnancy test at the end of the day, or even the fact that he wanted her to take one. She knew what it would say—she absolutely was not pregnant, so if he needed to see actual, real proof of that, then so be it.

She'd always been good at emptying her bladder on demand when she'd grown up with call times and marks to hit.

"I'll take the test, but you're damn well going to tell me why you acted the way you did about it," Vera stated, offering no room for argument.

"*Or. What.*"

She drew her line.

He'd not crossed it.

This time, Vera was the one who couldn't see the line he made for her to stay behind. A precarious game to play with Vaslav. He played to win, and for keeps.

"You'll sleep alone," Vera told him.

Vaslav scowled at the news, but at least, he kept his gaze averted while she peed. She continued, needing the steady stream of urine for three to five seconds on the end of the stick, to say, "And if you try any of that shit with me again, without at least the decency to explain what's triggered you so much, then the trip I take to my mother and father's this spring can be extended, Vaslav."

His jaw clenched.

"You didn't say *anything* about a trip to visit your parents in the spring," he muttered through tight teeth.

Yeah, well.

"I'm mentioning it now," Vera returned.

He finally turned his gaze back on her after the plastic test clattered to the countertop once she'd capped the grossest end. Finally, he seemed to put the issue of the pregnancy test out of his mind, and he didn't stare at it obsessively like before.

Not that his change in attitude helped how she felt.

"They're digital. Hannah couldn't be bothered with the regular ones, like she didn't already know what the answer would be when she's four days late, so we won't get an answer for least five minutes. It blinks *pregnant*," Vera said, shrugging, "Or not on the screen there."

She waved at the test, and then him. "Your turn."

"You really need to stop talking to Bogdan," Vaslav bitched under his breath. "I hate it when you use the words he does—*triggers*, and the rest ... it's not about—"

"Frankly, I'd like not to have to talk with your brain surgeon on a regular basis, either, but since he's the only human on earth with some form of a medical degree that you're willing to talk to, I've got to work with what I have, Vas."

There, she said it.

He wouldn't talk to a therapist, never mind a regular family physician who could just ask him simple questions once a week over the phone to monitor his symptoms that manifested as behaviors. Not all of them were good, productive, or healthy. It also took a great toll on his mental health, so Bogdan it was when things weren't great for Vaslav.

"Hannah's pregnant?" he asked, then, shuffling sideways so that his profile faced her where she shimmied her leggings and panties back up in place.

"Not that she wants to be," Vera confirmed, "but life happens."

Vaslav did little more than grunt under his breath at that statement. He eyed the bedroom space studiously instead of Vera once she was off the commode. Without explanation or warning, he walked out of sight, and Vera opted not to follow.

They both needed the space.

Unsurprisingly, his distance didn't last for long. Vaslav darkened the bathroom doorway once more, and tipped his head toward the pregnancy test on the counter while Vera washed her hands.

"What?" she asked.

"Toss it in the trash," he said, "and come with me."

Caught off-guard by the total one-eighty, Vera forgot to turn the taps off before she turned around with dripping wet hands. "For what?"

He sighed.

A heavy sound.

She saw how it weighed him down.

"Your answers," he said.

Before she could ask him to explain more, Vaslav disappeared out of view of the doorway again. She made quick work of turning off the taps, and grabbing the pregnancy test that she had no intention of throwing away like he said to. Stuffing it into the pocket of her oversized cardigan before she exited the bathroom, she stepped out to find Vaslav waiting at the doorway of the bedroom.

"Come on, it's in the safe."

"The safe?"

"In the den," he clarified.

Not once had he told her about a safe in the fucking den, and only now was the time he thought to do so. *Right*. Typical Vaslav. The whiplash this man gave her was unreal.

"And where is this safe in the den?" Vera asked.

Vaslav scratched at his jaw. "In and around, or under my desk."

"What?"

"What?" he parroted back.

Vera had caught onto that trick.
Even used it herself.
"Just show me the safe, Vas," she told him.
He led the way.

13.

Vera didn't quite know what to make of the large hole in the floor Vaslav had kept hidden with a simple rug she'd walked across more times than she cared to count. Never once did she notice that there might be something beneath it. Frankly, as Vaslav disappeared down the steps after he'd opened the hatch to the secret passageway down to his safe built under the floor, she wondered what else he had kept hidden in the house.

"Are there more?" Vera asked.

"More what?"

His voice echoed from inside the hole.

"Secret rooms, or—safes hidden under floors," Vera clarified.

Vaslav's steps came to a stop, but only briefly. He padded down the remaining stairs, but the pause in his reply told her what he would say before he could do it. "There may or may not be something that could be considered a safe room in the basement."

Vera's brow puckered with her contemplation. "May or may not be?"

"There is, it isn't particularly safe after eighteen or so hours. There's practically no air exchange down there. You'll slowly run out of oxygen. It's a last resort, yeah, but only if needed."

Well, then.

"Besides, I didn't have it installed to use myself—well," Vaslav added with a chuckle. "Not for my safety, no? It's been well-used, nonetheless."

There was something about the pleased cadence of his dark tone—twisting it in a joke she clearly couldn't understand—that kept Vera from asking more about the room in the basement. She had even less of a desire to know what he had used it for now.

"The panel mirror built into the wall in the room across from the den," Vaslav said.

Vera could visualize the decoration—strange to be at the far end of a small hallway in the large studio space—he talked about. "What about it?"

"That'll open up and take you down to it. If you can get the control panel to work."

Huh.

"Anything else?" Vera questioned.

"Not at the moment. I'll keep you informed."

Vaslav offered the news as if he already had something in mind that could soon come to fruition. What could she say to that?

The loud screech of metal against concrete sent Vera rising from the oyster-back decorative chair that typically sat unused in the corner of Vaslav's den. Standing gave her just enough room to see him at the bottom of the dark pit. While he'd turned on a handful of pot lights in the den, the main fixtures remained off, and kept the large space blanketed in shadows.

Nonetheless, she could see the door he'd pulled open. A door as large as he was tall, and at least six inches thick. Made of steel, the door couldn't be easy to pull back to expose what lay behind, but Vaslav did it without complaint.

Or even a grunt.

Hell, he couldn't carry on a conversation without tossing in one or two of those. Vera couldn't see from her position what he dug for at the very bottom of the large safe, but by the time he turned around, he didn't bother with closing the door before climbing the stairs.

At the top, he waved what he found.

A file.

All that work to move the chairs and desk, not to mention roll back the rug, for a legal-sized file he kept at the bottom of a safe under the floor. Did he have it like that so the work involved to get it to might deter himself, or someone else? Or was he just protecting what was inside the file? Knowing her husband the way she thought she did, Vera suspected his reasonings featured a bit of both things mixed together.

Vaslav waved the file, muttering, "Give me a minute. There's more than what I need here. It keeps everything else in one spot, yes?"

He wasn't looking for an actual response, so Vera took her seat once more in the chair in the corner while Vaslav headed for his desk. Once he sat behind the desk with the file open and a pile of papers spilled out, it was like the hole in the floor didn't exist.

Yet, Vera couldn't look away.

"I can't believe that's been here the whole time," she said.

"*Mmm.*" Vaslav sighed while discarding paper after paper in a second pile. "I emptied it last month. There's nothing very interesting or usable down there now. Maybe I'll build it back up, or maybe I won't."

"With what?"

Vaslav hesitated before discarding the next pile of papers that weren't what he was looking for, eventually saying, "Things."

"Helpful, Vas."

He shrugged. "It's not really for you."

Well, that was fair.

So, why worry about it?

A sigh from across the room—filled with more relief than his last—drew Vera's attention back to Vaslav. He extended his hand, a single piece of folded paper waiting for her to take if she felt like getting up from her chair. "Here it is—don't mind the rip, Irina didn't exactly intend on me finding it. She left it like that in the trash. I think she pulled it out of the fax too fast."

"Where was it faxed to?"

"Here," he answered. "The house. Two days before she died. The date's on the doctor's report. Take it and look for yourself."

Vera tried not to be too bothered by the large hole in the floor as she walked around it to retrieve the paper from Vaslav. As she did, she figured out what about it had her so … on edge. The hatch, although it opened from the top up, reminded her of the one that hadn't opened on stage for her during her last show.

At least, the trap door built into the stage hadn't opened when it was supposed to, and now, Vera was ignoring phantom pain in her ankle at just the thought alone because of the hole in Vaslav's floor. *Wonderful.*

Trauma could be a bitch.

Vaslav, not aware of Vera's inner war she wished didn't exist, kept a studious eye on her after she took the tri-folded paper, half ripped across the very middle, and opened it right where she stood next to his desk. His unrelenting gaze kept her hyperaware as she carefully opened the document—a mistake.

She couldn't hide the way her face fell.

Confused, her gaze skimmed down the doctor's report, addressed, dated, and signed by a physician with a name Vera recognized.

Not for a good reason, either.

"You see?" Vaslav asked.

She did.

She didn't *want* to.

Life had little care for her feelings—or so she had come to learn. The doctor's notes had also been short-hand written in English, so she couldn't mistake the news that had befallen Vaslav and his first wife just days before her murder.

"She was pregnant," Vera said, fainter than she wanted to.

Vaslav cleared his throat noisily, an attempt to gain her attention, but Vera could no longer look away from the paper—a fax, apparently, in her hands. "That last fight of ours—"

"You fought over this?"

Vaslav shook his head. "I found that after. She already knew; why else would she have gone in for the bloodwork, hmm?"

Vera shook her head. "I don't understand. You said

the fight—"

"At that time, to me, it was only a possibility."

Oh.

Her stare lifted from the paper, then, realizing how it must have felt for him to have fought with his wife about a possible pregnancy days before her death only to learn after it wasn't a possibility at all. And after she was gone, well, it would never be a possibility again.

To have something, and then lose it—only to get it back but still be giving it away; grief like that could tear a soul apart.

Vera saw how it left Vaslav's soul tired and tattered.

"You blew up a doctor's office because they faxed a positive pregnancy result to your wife two days before she died?" Vera asked quietly.

She needed to ask it under her breath—like she was trying to give him the option to pretend he didn't hear it—because she was scared of the answer. All the information Vera had managed to gather about Vaslav's past was never far from her mind, even if the two didn't talk about it. That was by his choice; her only option was to deal with it.

"Her private doctor," Vaslav clarified. Then, his tone and brow lifted when he added, "A *friend*, really."

"What does that mean? Why did you say it like that with your whole face just—"

His fist slammed sideways into the desk with a snap. "I loved my wife, Vera!"

The yell, mostly just his raised voice from clearly being overwhelmed, silenced Vera instantly. Sometimes, she'd noticed that when high emotions were involved, it took Vaslav practically no time at all to get frustrated as he tried to talk. His way of dealing with that was getting louder.

To anyone who had knowledge of Vaslav's violent background, his sudden bouts of aggression could be frightening or a warning.

His size alone meant when he was loud, *everyone* was sure to hear it.

Vera had to remind herself that she couldn't shrink under Vaslav the same way the rest of the world did because she wasn't scared of him. "You know, if you let people have more than ten minutes in a room with you, it's not hard to figure out how to avoid shit like this. If you need a second, then take it. You dumped a lot on me with this."

Across the desk, her husband cocked his eyebrow in challenge. "You dropped a lot on me upstairs."

She heaved a breath.

"Yeah, you're right," she returned.

Even if she didn't entirely understand why yet.

Vera placed the old fax back to Vaslav's desk while he left his chair and headed for the wet bar. Only stocked with bottles used for decoration, and some wine Vera liked, he opted for the pitcher of fresh water that Mira kept stocked and chilled every couple of hours. Except in the evenings. She filled it one last time, and she went back in the morning. He didn't have a complaint to make about the probably lukewarm water after downing a good half of a glass.

"Do you know why I really don't want you to meet my mother?" Vaslav asked, smacking what water remained from his lips as he turned to Vera.

"Because she's sick; you've cut her from your life, and—"

"She tormented Irina," Vaslav interjected, more

amused in his tone than Vera thought he should be considering the subject.

"Excuse me?"

Vaslav rolled his eyes, and after setting the glass upside down on the bar top the moveable wetbar, explained, "My apologies—it sounds heartless, yes? I sound heartless."

"Well …"

"Irina tormented her right back; they enjoyed it. I was a year into my marriage when my mother looked at me and remarked how boys married their mothers. I couldn't forget it. I wish I had paid more attention when she said it. There's a lot of history with this, some I can't even remember that explains what I'm trying to convey here, but—" Vaslav sucked in a deep breath at the sudden cut off of his ramblings, and squeezed his eyes shut.

Vera didn't move a muscle.

She didn't even breathe.

"I didn't make that same mistake a second time around, and I want you to know that first before anything else, Vera," he said.

"But what does any of this have to do with what I asked?"

"*Vera,*" Vaslav said sharply, his eyes snapping open to land on her with enough heat to silence her questioning. "You're not a replacement for Irina. You're not her, and to me, you'll never be. I didn't make the same mistake my mother saw before I did, okay? I didn't do that this time."

His plea made her listen.

She nodded. "Okay."

"I didn't blow up a fucking doctor's office because I knew the pregnancy existed; I did it so no one else would. It wasn't mine, and Irina was already dead, so why give my mother fodder to disgrace a dead woman? I already had plans for the reason why it happened."

Vera blinked.

Only a handful of things happened because of Vaslav after Irina's murder.

"Do you mean her father—"

"I beat my head into the white cement brick of my isolation room thirteen times before I finally knocked myself out on the first night my mother succeeded in getting me locked in that fucking asylum," Vaslav muttered through a thick, audible swallow. "As much as everybody just saw me as fucking crazy, I needed it all out of my head."

"The only thing I wanted to forget when I woke up—see, it didn't take me a long time to learn how my memories were gone after concussions—it didn't even matter, I haven't been able to forget that. What they all did to me. This fucking disease is gonna take everything, and everyone else, from me before I can let go of those memories. And when it doesn't," he said, pointing at the folded, ripped paper where Vera left it, "... when there's days that shit's fuzzy, and I need to put together this goddamn picture in my head, I've got enough to do that."

Vera's gaze drifted to the desk. "The whole file?"

He had one on her, too.

She didn't ask about it, though.

Vaslav rubbed the pads of his fingers roughly into his eye sockets. "Not even the weed is helping with this."

"Stop that, you know it doesn't even help," she warned.

His hands slapped to his thighs, and he glared at her from the side. Not that it bothered Vera.

"How did you know it wasn't yours?" she asked. Before she lost the nerve.

"I'd not touched her in almost three months," Vaslav said, a hand cutting through the air as if to wipe the words away as soon as he said them. Not that they could be. "Too long—she would have at least been starting to show. Business kept me away, but Vera, I wasn't faithful, either. That's a different mess ..."

"And a different man," Vera noted.

Or that's what it sounded like to her.

His shoulders dropped a bit as they loosened, but it was only enough to make him appear tired. She bet he was.

"Who do you talk to about stuff like this, Vas?"

"I don't want to—that's the point," he muttered.

Vera, still vibrating with nervous energy and a new ache in her heart, could no longer stand where she did. So far away from him. Once she was tucked into his chest, bearhugged in his trembling arms, she barely had room to breathe.

Who needed air?

She understood now why little lies or even hiding something could be the tip of a much bigger, and dangerous iceberg for Vaslav. How pregnancy tests could upset his entire evening if he had nothing but himself to confide in.

Who else listened?

Who really *knew*?

When he told her that he didn't think she was the same as Irina, that he hadn't made the same mistake, Vera hadn't truly realized what he was telling her. Not until that moment, smothered in the warmth of him.

"I want to go to bed," he told her. "I don't have to think about those things so much when I'm with you. I almost forget them completely sleeping next to you."

It wasn't even late enough for the sky to have darkened.

She wasn't at all tired.

None of that mattered.

Vera couldn't think of one other thing she would rather do.

14.

For the first time ever, Vera rang the doorbell on her villa, and even knocked on the window glass of the front door just to make sure the person inside heard that someone was waiting outside. Not because she couldn't just use the spare on her keyring—the only extra key that she knew of except for the one Hannah now used. Hannah wouldn't care if Vera just walked in and announced her surprise arrival, but the noise she heard coming from inside the villa as she walked up the steps to where the familiar welcome mat waited to greet her.

"You know what, fuck you, too, Mom."

Hannah hadn't shouted again after Vera made herself known at the front door. In fact, when her friend pulled the brown door open, she didn't even have a phone in her hand. The corner of the sleek, black device peeked out of the pocket of Hannah's pink, oversized cardigan.

No smile waited for Vera.

Hannah didn't even look happy to see her.

"What's wrong?" Vera asked.

Visibly, her friend's shoulders dropped a good inch or two. "Since when do you ring the doorbell and knock like that? It's *your* house."

"So?"

Hannah let out a shaky gust of breath, and raked a hand through the frizzy curls she had tossed high in a messy bun.

"I heard you on the phone with your mom," Vera admitted when Hannah couldn't hold her gaze across the threshold for more than two entire seconds. "And I was trying to make it less awkward because I didn't even call to tell you I was going to come to the city and spend a night with you."

"Maybe a call might have been nice."

Yeah.

The way Hannah hugged her cardigan closer to her body, using her own arms to hug around her thin frame, told Vera a lot. It had been one too many days since she called to check in on Hannah after she left the house in Dubna. Vera took the blame for that entirely.

Sometimes, her husband just took up all the space in her head and life. All a once, too. He needed that unbridled, unapologetic attention from her, though, so she couldn't regret or change that she might be spacey at times. A couple or a few days without a phone call could happen more often than it didn't.

Not that knowing as much helped with her guilt.

Not at the moment when her best friend wiped at her eyes with the heels of her palms like she was a breath away from crying. Clearly, the news of Hannah's pregnancy had not landed well, and she suffered for it.

That's not how this should be.

Vera stepped over the ledge at the bottom of the door, and wrapped her friend in a tight hug right where they stood. Cold air rushed in through the open doorway, but neither of the two women bothered to close it. The entire street could see them embracing, or the way Hannah's shoulders had started to tremble the second Vera hugged her, but none of that mattered.

"It's okay," she told Hannah the longer they lingered in the chilly entry of the villa.

The cold wasn't good for the plants, either, but a few minutes wouldn't do any damage to the hanging pots of vines in the hallway.

"It'll be okay," Vera corrected when Hannah sniffled, and still didn't relent in the way she hugged back like a lifeline in a raging storm. Vera could be the lifeline. Her own issue—the reason why she'd made the surprise trip—could wait a bit longer.

Mumbled against Vera's neck, her friend admitted the real reason for her current emotional state and why her phone call had gotten loud enough for people walking by the villa to hear.

"She said she'd pay for it."

Vera almost didn't hear Hannah.

Except she had.

"Pay for what?" she asked.

Not that she really needed to. Vera was almost positive of the thing her friend alluded to without needing all the details. She still wanted confirmation that Hannah's mother, instead of choosing kindness and compassion for the situation her daughter found herself in, instead opting to pile more pain on top of an unplanned pregnancy.

"The abortion," Hannah whispered.

Yeah.

Fuck.

Vera couldn't imagine those words coming from the mouth of her own mother, and the flinch that raced down her body—secondhand pain from Hannah that she could feel soaking through to her—left her anger simmering all at once.

"I'm sorry," she repeated again.

Hannah deserved to hear it, even if no one else had the nerve to say it.

"She's gonna cut me off," Hannah said, shrugging like it might make the reality facing her disappear. "Starting next month, I guess. If I don't—"

"She's not really going to do that to you. Because you're *pregnant?*"

Vera couldn't wrap her mind around that. She was just self-aware enough to comprehend that her own loving parents gave her a different experience and outlook on parenthood and what it meant than what others had to live through.

Look at Vaslav.

He hated his mother; swore to the heavens that she despised him, too, and that's how his own hatred had started. How could a parent look in the face of their child and treat them like trash—important and useless?

How?

Hannah stepped around Vera to swing the front door closed. Once it latched shut, she sighed and said, "No, she will, because she knows it'll work. Or she thinks it'll work," Hannah corrected, wincing at her mistake. "I'm not going to kill my baby just because she's pissed off that I won't tell her who the father is, and I won't move back to Italy where I can—*once again*—be under her thumb twenty-four seven."

Vera cringed. "She did help you with Viktor."

"And it came at a cost," Hannah returned. "My dignity. A lot of pride. Do you think it was any better for me to listen to her verbally abuse me day after day as opposed to Viktor hitting me every time I turned around?"

Vera knew Hannah also hadn't been given much of a choice. At the time, her mother was the only person in her life with any money and influence to help her out of the bad situation with her ex-husband. Not all sacrifices made a person grow.

Hannah shrugged. "It still hurts, Vera. Abuse is all the same. It still *kills*."

"People who can't love themselves shouldn't have kids," Vera muttered, the first thing flying through her mind to also leave her lips. "How can they love their kids if they can't even feel that way about the person creating the baby? It's not like an actual child that depends on you to live for the first two decades of their life is going to fix all the things wrong in someone's life, and then what happens? People put all their pain and trauma into littler people who grow up to have bigger problems because of it."

A whole *cycle*.

It wouldn't end.

Hannah stayed quiet during Vera's rant.

"Sorry," she muttered to her friend after. "It's a little close to home."

Hannah raised a brow in question. "What, *your* mom and dad are—"

"No, but someone else has a not-so-great

relationship with his mother, and things have happened because of that lately."

A lame explanation, but Vera wouldn't offer more on the topic.

Hannah's crinkled nose and puckered brow spoke of her confusion. "Do you mean your husband?"

Vera sighed. "It just seems to be a theme, okay? Shitty parents who don't love themselves or their kids who make grown people that don't know or can't manage or even understand a lot of what they feel. I'm just saying, I've noticed it."

"Right," Hannah returned.

Not like she believed it.

Vera waved a hand, and started to pull the messenger bag from her shoulder. She had yet to even kick off her boots or remove her coat, and they hadn't even left the entry of the villa."

"I also have practically no money without the accounts and credit cards she gives me access to," Hannah added while Vera hung her bag and coat on a hook in the hallway. She turned to face Hannah who had chosen the floor to study. "Everything I did have, Viktor took. I didn't even get a high school diploma out of The Swan House. She pulled the right ropes, Vera—if she cuts them, I drown."

"Money is the last thing you need to worry about. I've got three cards in my wallet, and you could take any of them for six months before Vaslav would notice it probably wasn't me spending the money."

That was a lie.

Her husband was too obsessive with tracking their financials, even if she had an all-access pass to the wealth that was now under her name. Nonetheless, she seriously doubted Vaslav would say shit to her handling her friend's affairs for a while. A few hundred thousand, likely less, to help Hannah get on her feet and have a healthy, *loved* baby was nothing. A drop in the bucket to the billions upon billions of bloodstained money that belonged to her.

Or so the paperwork said.

No matter.

Vaslav wouldn't care. He had so much money, and had become accustomed to that wealth in such a way that he barely thought about it. He wouldn't run out. Their proverbial bank account was a bottomless pit.

He *would* notice the spending, however—and Vera could deal with that. Nonetheless … he wouldn't care. Hell, he'd paid his mother to keep her under control for years.

Hannah scratched at the base of her neck, saying, "I don't want to take your money."

"It's not taking my money. I'm giving it."

That ended that. Vera didn't bother to explain how, eventually, a certain business in the city that meant a great deal to both her and Hannah would also belong to her. She had plans for The Swan House, selfishly selfless and beautiful dreams that she didn't even dare speak about yet. Those same plans and dreams would someday benefit Hannah, too.

Official notices from estate barristers had come through on papers with all the legal letterheads attached at the top—her own lawyer, compliments of a legal team she hadn't even realized Vaslav kept on the payroll, stepped in to handle the middleman details.

Vera never saw a cop.

Didn't speak to a *musor.*

In fact, if she didn't occasionally see the marked

and unmarked vehicles—although, still obvious by their blacked-out windows and attached lights—she wouldn't know police even existed in her world. Never mind captains and detectives piecing together an already cold crime scene.

Feliks' body still had not been found.

Vaslav had been right—it was all a waiting game.

"I'm finally learning how to drive the Hummer, by the way, but I called the car service for a driver this week. Maybe next, I'll try the trip myself."

Unlikely.

Vera was a big fan of wishful thinking.

"And?" Hannah asked.

"I'm trying to change the subject so you'll stop looking so sad for a minute. Don't let what other people think or feel about your pregnancy ruin the way you smiled when I told you all the tests were positive."

Hannah let out a little laugh.

Weak as it was …

Vera shrugged one shoulder, smiling a bit herself. "I know you were scared, and you didn't even want to tell anybody right away, but a part of you was happy, too. That's what your baby deserves. For their mother to just be happy."

Hannah's shoulders lifted and dropped with the weight of her next breath. "Yeah, I'm trying."

"Did you tell Igor yet?"

The expression darkening Hannah's face told Vera the answer. She had not.

"Not for lack of trying," Hannah explained. "He hasn't called me in a week, and that last time we spoke … I get the impression he's busy, but it's not like he told me with what. So, I left a few messages.

He's supposed to come around tonight."

Shit.

Guilt gnawed harder on Vera's soul.

"I really should have called first, huh?"

Hannah shrugged, helpless but smiling.

A little.

"It's all right," she said.

"I can stay out of sight, keep my headphones in, yadda yadda," Vera replied. "Unless you want me to go, I can call the car—"

"No, I want you to stay. Did you at least give Vaslav more heads up than me?" Hannah asked.

That was where things got tricky.

"I did," Vera replied.

Carefully.

Hannah hadn't missed it.

"Why did you say it like that?"

It was that moment when Vera decided it was time to share her own secret. Reaching into the messenger bag she had hung earlier on the wall, she produced the remaining unopened pregnancy test that had been left over.

Hannah squinted at the test. "I think it's too late for another one of—"

"It's for me," Vera interrupted. "I came here to take it."

All at once, Hannah's jaw fell open.

Flies could have made a home.

Vera chewed on her bottom lip, eyeing the pink and white box with the strangest anxiety growing in her chest from deep inside her heart. "Vaslav found the tests," she explained, "and made me take one. Not long after you left, actually. We had a fight, I had put the test in my pocket—"

"Was it positive?" Hannah asked.

"Did you miss the part where he *made* me take a test?"

"I figured he must have thought they were yours," Hannah replied. "I mean, if I was a guy and I thought my wife was pregnant with my kid but was hiding it, I would want to know, too."

How simple.

Would every man overreact as much as Vaslav had? Vera didn't quite think so, but it was a distinction she couldn't make for Hannah without explaining the why for said reaction, too. So, she did neither.

"He did think they were mine. We don't want kids, Hannah."

She didn't explain why. That was too deep.

Vera got it, though.

She understood.

Vaslav, so hated by his own mother, who also hated her, came from a long line of the same history cycling again and again. He didn't want to be a father if he thought there was a chance he would be a bad one, but he had too much pride to say as much. Even so, he had a right to make that choice.

No judgement stared back from Hannah. Just solemn stillness that made Vera feel heard and understood.

"The test he made me take …" Vera trailed off, knowing what came next wouldn't sound good. She had to get it out, though. Someone except her needed to *know*. "I didn't check it for a couple of hours, and by then, you couldn't even read the screen. I was two weeks late for my last shot; three times last week, I smelled something cooking and almost didn't make it to the bathroom before I puked. And *look*."

Lifting the hoodie she wore, Vera peeled up the shirt underneath for her friend to see the way her breasts seemed to overfill her sports bras lately. She wasn't ashamed of Hannah seeing her body; they spent years dancing and training side by side, changing from one outfit or costume to another. Modesty was the least of Vera's problems.

"They hurt, too," Vera added.

Just to make the point clear.

Hannah cringed. "Yikes."

"I'm probably pregnant," Vera said.

And lucky her husband had not yet noticed the few, subtle changes. Mostly because he spent a good portion of the last couple of weeks in bed, the migraines coming and going without any real ease to his constant suffering.

"I just need to know," Vera said. "If I am, I want to know for sure. Then, I'll tell Vas."

They could deal with what it all meant later.

For one single second, though, Vera *needed* to be absolutely sure. So be it if it was selfish, she also needed to know it when she was alone.

Hannah sucked in air through her teeth like a hiss. "Oh, wow."

Yep.

That sentiment worked just as well, too.

"It's a bit of a mess, I guess," Vera said.

Understatement.

"What are we gonna do?" Hannah asked.

15.

It's easy, Vera's inner monologue ran inside her head. *Come on, do it.* A constant streaming loop of the same thoughts over and over, because frankly, *she* wasn't wrong. This was easy. It wasn't even the first time she'd done this very thing. Her thoughts ripped through her self-awareness with another line of instructions she should be able to follow through: *Just take the fucking pregnancy test.*

Yet, she couldn't follow through.

Vera remained frozen on the toilet seat that had long since turned warm with her ass sitting on it. All the while, she couldn't bear to rip her gaze away from the pregnancy test that sat on the sink directly across from her. Balancing precariously on the edge of the sink bowl, the cap side facing her, the test sat unused.

Early morning, muted daylight filtered in through the privacy frosted glass of the windows framing both sides of the mirror that Vera stared into—the face staring back, emotionless and paralyzed, didn't entirely feel like her own.

She blinked.

The reflection blinked back.

Bathed in soft yellow warmth from the sunlight, one of her favorite features of the downstairs bathroom in the villa, she was still a little cold.

A knock on the other side of the bathroom door had Vera jerking out of her zoning as Hannah's voice filtered through the painted white wood. "Did you do it yet?"

Vera let out a gusty breath, but it did nothing to soothe her frazzled nerves. She called back to her friend, "No."

"You couldn't take it yesterday, or last night, either."

After releasing her last breath, Vera forgot to take another in until her lungs burned, and she opened her mouth wide to swallow a gulp of air that didn't help until she'd taken a few more. Hannah's reminder wasn't needed; Vera knew good and well how obvious her cowardice was in that moment.

It changed nothing.

She still couldn't take the test.

"I think I made a mistake," Vera told the empty bathroom.

Too low for Hannah to hear on the other side of the thick door, or maybe her friend would have heard if she didn't have her own pile of issues to currently deal with.

"So hey, Igor's about to head out, and I want to say goodbye," Hannah said, her voice slightly more muffled as she tampered her tone.

Vera didn't feel any particular way about the news, and she'd done exactly what she'd promised to the night before when Igor showed up behind the wheel of his familiar SUV. She stayed out of sight, didn't intrude upstairs while the two had their conversations … or *whatever*.

She even pretended like she didn't hear that bit, too.

By the time morning arrived, Vera had barely slept a wink, and the unused pregnancy test had not been far from her mind. Especially when her husband sent a morning greeting that proclaimed he both missed her, and didn't sleep well, either.

The knife of guilt stabbed deeper.

"Vera?" Hannah called. "Did you hear me?"

"Yeah," she replied before Hannah spent one more second worrying about Vera's selfish foolishness. She was a grown woman who made *grown* choices; these were simply the consequences, and now she had to deal with them. "Go say goodbye, Hannah, I hope you guys got everything figured out."

"Uh, yeah," her friend mumbled almost too low for Vera to hear. "Something like that. We can talk about it later. You know, after he's gone."

"Sure, right."

Vera couldn't hear Hannah's retreat down the hall, but she did get a whisper of relief at the idea she was once again alone.

If you're pregnant—

Her thoughts always shut off at that point in the question. Like her mind couldn't wrap around moving further. If she was pregnant, *what?*

That was the thing.

The struggle.

Her reason for all of this.

She couldn't answer that one question.

As quickly as being alone had brought her a sense of relief, it soon took her back to the cold grip of emptiness. Something she recognized came from the fact that she had waited almost two entire weeks to take the pregnancy test in her hand. She'd pretended as if it wasn't a question hanging in the air over her head. She lied by omission every time she had a conversation with Vaslav because the knowledge of what might be stayed stuck to the back of her mind. There was no escape.

Now here she was.

Alone in a bathroom.

Simply thinking: *This is not where I want to be.* Or perhaps, in her heart she knew, this wasn't where she should be.

Yet, having that awareness of where she should be—at home with her husband to do this—it didn't change where she was. Never mind the fact that Vera couldn't stand the idea of going one more second not knowing if she was pregnant.

The universe had a funny way of working. The second she reached for the test, the pressing urge of her bladder making itself known with sharp pangs, her phone beeped and the screen lit up with a blink of light. Not far away from where the pregnancy test sat on the rim of the sink, the phone laid on the counter around the elevated bowl.

Considering she'd been holding in her pee so that she didn't waste the morning urine—the best to take the test—and she'd already yanked down her panties before sitting on the toilet, she had to make a conscious effort to keep the stream back.

While she checked her phone.

More surprising was the notification that waited for

167

her on the screen. A request from a contact for a video call.

Vaslav.

That wasn't like him at all. He did well to text, preferring a call more than anything else when he did want to talk on the phone. His ever-present paranoia didn't allow him much more, and Vera tried more often than not to keep that in mind when all she wanted to do was check in throughout the day if she wasn't at home with him.

Nonetheless, the opportunity was prime.

She couldn't pass it up.

The simple request for a video call was the proverbial olive branch to correct every mistake Vera had made up until that moment regarding her new secret, and she grasped to it like a lifeline. She unlocked the phone, and accepted the request for a video chat, slipping her index finger through the ring handle to stabilize her video and give the camera a better angle.

Vaslav answered the call where he laid in bed, according to the slightly pixelated background. "Oh, that is how that works, yes?"

Vera smiled. "A video call?"

"I wondered if that's what that icon did when I clicked on it."

"You were just staring at my contact card wondering what the different icons did?"

"It's a new phone," he returned.

Only a little defensive.

She had been the one to pick up his newest burner device from a shop in Dubna that promised to keep extra stock on hand of whatever phone her husband preferred. It simply took her last name and the address of where the phones should be delivered for the man who ran the shop to understand the important person he was dealing with.

It was Vera's first time realizing how well-known her husband actually was in the area. Being told was not the same as experiencing it firsthand.

On the screen, Vaslav squinted one eye where his head was half smooshed into a grey pillow. She could only see the unscarred side of his face, but when she blinked had had her eyes closed for a brief half of a second, she could map the rest of his expression from memory.

"I wasn't lying this morning when I said I missed you," he told her. "Maybe I knew what the icon was for, hmm?"

"I wasn't entirely honest, either," she returned.

His partially amused expression bled away any fondness that had been staring at her. In its place was his puckered brow and confusion. "What?"

A reasonable question.

Now or never.

There was no going back.

She snatched the pregnancy test off the counter at the same time she told Vaslav, "The first pregnancy test I took—" Her words cut off when it appeared like Vaslav was lifting out of bed, and the phone rolled into the blankets, leaving the screen black for a few seconds. Once she could see him again, although it appeared like he was now sitting up in bed, Vera continued. "I waited too long to get an accurate result I could read."

She produced what she'd been hiding in her hand, making the pregnancy test visible to her husband. Yet, his stony gaze didn't flicker a bit on the screen to say the plastic pink and white test had taken any of his interest or attention.

His silence was the worst, though.

It made her keep talking.

Just so someone was saying *something*.

"I still thought—I was sure—I wasn't pregnant, but I didn't—"

"You went to Hannah's to take the pregnancy test?"

"Yes, but no I haven't taken it yet," Vera admitted. "I couldn't do it. I felt too guilty. Like I was lying to you—hiding something from you. And knowing what I do …" She trailed off, lifting one shoulder as his expression fell with sadness, and he glanced downward at something she couldn't see on the screen.

"I noticed some other things; I got sick, too, and—"

"Would you take it now?" he asked.

The request was quite different from the first time he demanded it of her. She didn't even verbally agree, and just popped off the cap carelessly. It fell to the floor, bouncing alongside the toilet where she could retrieve it later.

"Might be easier if you don't listen," Vera said. "There's a mute—"

"Really, I don't think you can use that excuse. We've done this once," Vaslav returned, mustering one of his cocky grins for her on the screen. All the while, her hand trembled while she grasped onto the pregnancy test. There, it sat so lightly, yet it still weighed her down with an unseen heaviness from the what ifs she couldn't answer.

"Besides," her husband added, clearing his throat,

"in ten or fifteen years, I won't even be walking to the bathroom. Let's not get ahead of ourselves in complaining now."

"You'll have a nurse."

Several, if needed. No matter the state of him, he would be taken care of, and she was going to make sure of it. Maybe she didn't have a realistic look at what that future would be, but she wasn't living in delusions, either.

Vaslav grunted while Vera placed the phone on the counter so she could see him, and he had a view of her from the neck up. Neither of them spoke while the tinkling tell-tale sound hit the water in the ceramic bowl. Vera grabbed the cap from the floor and pulled the test from between her legs while she finished relieving her poor bladder.

"Do you want to have a child to raise and me to manage in ten years, as well?" Vaslav questioned.

Focused on pulling her panties up and resituating on the toilet after she flushed it, Vera hadn't been expecting his frank question. She froze as she was sitting down, the pause noticeable between the period she remained in the air to when her backside fell. He didn't give her the chance to think of what she wanted to say before he spoke again, not that she had the words, anyway.

"When you can't keep the doors unlocked because I'll forget my way outside, and I barely even remember the halls inside this house anymore, do you want a child then? When can they ever be loud? Stampede over the floors? Don't they cry for the first few years of their godforsaken lives? Do you want a child to manage between my fits and *pain* and—"

"It's not really about a baby," she told him,

stopping his rant in its tracks.

He couldn't deny it.

He didn't even try.

Vaslav's Adam's apple bobbed with his next swallow, and he rubbed at the pinch between his brows with the heel of his palm. "Say you're right, yes? Let us say that this way I feel isn't really about a child that doesn't even exist. Vera, *love* … my *kisska*, I barely like the person staring back at me in the mirror. You're asking a lot of me to think I'll muster more for another living, breathing part of me."

He laughed, and the sound cut her deep. There was something about the way he seemed to honestly believe that even his own child would represent pain for him.

"And who's to say that they would even like me?" he asked quietly.

Only he could determine that, but she didn't think Vaslav needed her to point it out. Nor would he appreciate it if she compared his many overarching contradictions or inconsistencies. Her husband was far from a stupid man. Before anything he said ever left his lips, he'd already repeated them to himself silently at least ten times.

Hearing something—whether it was ridiculous or nonsensical—didn't actually change how Vaslav felt about it, or the way he perceived his beliefs about a topic.

"Where's Hannah?" Vaslav asked.

"Saying goodbye to Igor."

She didn't glance up from the test on her lap to see how Vaslav reacted to the news, but his noise of interest told her more than enough.

"He's not once mentioned to me that Hannah is

pregnant."

"You didn't ask?"

"I'm not really the type," her husband replied.

Vera wished she could muster up some quip to make Vaslav laugh about his surly personality, but her gaze remained down on the pregnancy test she'd balanced on her bare thigh.

"It's been two minutes, no?" Vaslav asked.

Like he *knew*.

Time was up.

"It started blinking before the timer on the screen finished counting down," Vera informed.

"You're pregnant."

"I already called the car service. I'll be home by noon."

"Vera, just say it—you're pregnant."

That's what he wanted? For her to say it? It wouldn't make anything better. It wouldn't change a thing about what he'd said to her.

Fine.

She'd say it.

"Yeah, Vas, I'm pregnant."

Vera couldn't say what she expected to follow the news. Her husband, prone to a variety of reactions, remained frozen on the screen in that moment. A second before the loudest boom she'd ever heard practically knocked her off the toilet seat and into the cabinetry in front of her.

She thought she blacked out.

The dust following a sudden unexplainable heat and a chill from icy wind as Vera blinked up at the bright sky overhead proved her consciousness, but knowledge of the state did little to help Vera roll over from her back, or explain where the walls and roof had gone.

Over distant screams, blaring vehicle alarms, the woosh of spraying water, and the crackle of wood, Vera heard something else.

Vaslav.

He called for her.

She just couldn't answer him back.

Vera was barely able to breathe, but she remembered taking one more breath before everything went black.

16.

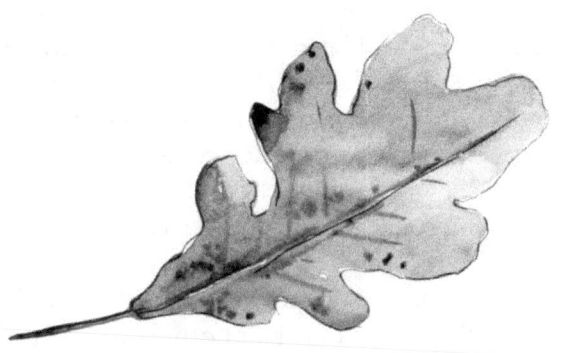

Vaslav's shoes crunched along the ashy debris that remained on the walkway. Debris that would soon be cleaned away. The remnants of his wife's old villa was a ghost of what it used to be. Two weeks after the bomb, and the bones of what had once been the rear bottom half of Vera's villa was all that was left standing in the backdrop of darkness.

They let it burn for hours, or so he was told. What bit had caught fire, anyway. It left the rubble to smolder and smoke for days, even in the cold. He couldn't help but picture the way the yellow walls of the villa had looked greeting him, and how Vera's front door was now just a gaping hole in the darkness.

Her home.

Their child.

Gone.

Vaslav was intimately acquainted with the way life could change in a split second, but that didn't make the rollercoaster trip through hell any easier to deal with. If anything, he thought knowing so well how these things tended to play out made him angrier and more anxious than ever.

Violent, too.

Most of the front of the villa, including the steps, walls, and rooms had been taken out by the bomb someone had planted in Igor's car. The night before the blast, everyone presumed. It wasn't like there were very many people whom Vaslav could ask for answers.

Hannah, medically induced into a coma to help her recover while recurrent swelling in her brain continued to lead her through dangerous medical events—well, she certainly had nothing to say. Igor, burned and medicated, likely the closest to the blast, had more bandages than skin at the moment. He also wasn't in the mood to talk.

And *Vera* ...

"I can confirm the blast was triggered by the unlocking system." The politsiya constable just a few steps ahead of Vaslav pulled his standard uniform, fur cap from his head and swatted his thigh to dust off the stray snowflakes. "Some wires and a box were found still attached to a part of the fuse panel. It didn't take long to match what part of the car that belonged to, and so—"

"Once the unlock button was pressed on the fob, *boom.*"

"*Da.*"

All that money he paid to the officials to get a record of the investigative side of things, and *that* was what the constable called him from his wife's hospital bedside to tell him? A theory he had already figured out on his own because of his basic understanding of where and how the three people on the property had been found?

Vera, in the far downstairs bathroom.

Hannah, where she had been blown back to the far end of the entry hall. Only Igor had been outside. As the bomb had been pretty obviously connected to the mob, given it was placed on Igor's unwatched vehicle—a *stupid* move for such a smart man—the *musor* and any other detective or cop looking for information already knew they would have to come up with it on their own.

Nobody talked.

Nobody knew a thing.

As to be expected.

"A waste of my fucking time," Vaslav muttered in Russian, turning to head back for the street where his black Hummer waited with the lights on at all four points of the vehicle. He'd left it running with the lights on because he couldn't care less if the neighbors were watching.

Let the whole city watch.

The beast was back on the warpath.

"Mr. Pashkov," the constable called at Vaslav's retreating back, "don't you have something for me?"

"The money was enough."

"You promised information!"

Tit for tat.

The cop jumped at the chance.

"I lied," he returned dryly as his shoes crunched on the clean snow of the sidewalk.

The thing was, Vaslav also had little to nothing that he was able to tell. He didn't have the first clue who planted the bomb, *why*, or how he could deal with it. Not that he should. The retirement was still in place, a living, breathing Igor meant the Russian bratva still had a head at the top of the organization to answer to, and it wasn't Vaslav.

Not anymore.

It couldn't be if he intended to keep his hands clean, and remain an observer of that criminal underworld from a safe distance. Except it could never be safe.

Wasn't this proof?

"*Vaslav Pashkov!*" the officer shouted at him.

He barked out a laugh.

The man thought using his full first name would make a difference, but it did nothing in the end. Vaslav didn't so much as glance over his shoulder as he crossed the street to where his idling Hummer waited. The constable hadn't even moved from his spot where the steps to Vera's villa had once been by the time Vaslav sat behind the driver's wheel.

Glaring, the man across the street waved his fur cap furiously at the vehicle.

Vaslav rolled down the tinted windows to make sure the constable had an unobstructed view of him, and then he stuck up a middle finger back.

"Nice," came the mutter from the backseat of the Hummer.

Vaslav ignored Kiril.

"Stupid prick," he uttered under his breath while he yanked the vehicle out of park.

Not about the teenager who had become his new, and unfortunate, companion over the last couple of weeks. Circumstances brought the two together, and Vaslav hadn't been given much of a choice when he found Kiril sleeping in his car in the hospital parking lot three nights after the bomb. In the middle of fucking winter.

Mira wouldn't have forgiven him had he left the teenager to fend for himself even though Vaslav knew Kiril was perfectly capable, and had done so for a long time.

Neither would Vera.

That's who Vaslav really cared about.

"He's definitely considering having you arrested," Kiril said as Vaslav let his tires squeal on the wet, cold asphalt as he did a U-turn in the middle of the street.

"On *what?* Fuck him. I'll burn his house to the ground if I see his fucking face again."

The whole lot of them.

Every musor in this city.

And every *vor*, too.

No one was safe.

Vaslav would figure out how this happened on his own seeing as how everybody else was clearly useless. A shame, really. Nobody seemed to like the way he did things.

Too bad for them.

They all had their chance.

*

"I'm *fine*, Papa. I can't help that Vaslav won't answer your calls or return them. He barely returns mine ..." Vera's assurances for her father trailed off just long enough for her to let out a sigh. "That's ridiculous. You're being ridiculous."

Vaslav decided that was the moment to make his presence known to his wife. Whoever had been last to leave her private hospital room left the door open a couple of inches. Just enough to allow someone outside in the hallway to eavesdrop.

Him, unfortunately.

Pushing the door open, earning him a swing of Vera's head as he entered the room, Vaslav asked, "What is Demyan saying that's so ridiculous, hmm?"

The smile that fettered across his wife's lips as she saw him was short lived. But only because she had to return to the conversation with the man on the other end of the phone.

"Yes, Papa, that's him." Vera rolled her eyes Vaslav's way, and rubbed at her cheek with her IV-connected hand. A friend she would hopefully be rid of soon if everything went well over the next couple of days. Or so her doctor said when Vaslav cornered the man in the carpark that morning. "If he hasn't picked up your calls yet, then I think we can both assume he doesn't want to talk to you n—"

"Give me that, *spasibo*," Vaslav said, arriving at Vera's bedside and pulling the phone out of her hand before she could finish her defense of him. He appreciated it, but now wasn't the right time. A worried Demyan was low on Vaslav's list of priorities, but he could appreciate that Vera was high on her father's list, respectively.

They wanted the same thing.

Essentially.

"Demyan," Vaslav greeted as he put the phone to his ear.

"Imagine I'm having a conversation with my injured, hospitalized daughter, and *now* is the time you decide is the best to take a fucking phone call from me," Demyan returned, hotly.

It was due.

Vaslav didn't correct the man.

"*Da*, well," Vaslav muttered, lamely. "There are only so many hours in the day, Demyan."

"You said she was safe."

That accusation, not nearly as angry but still heavy, sent Vaslav glancing Vera's way as he rounded the foot of her bed, but she only glowered back at him. Obviously, she wasn't happy about his trick with her phone. The room wasn't much bigger than the first she'd had in the same hospital two wings over, but it had a television.

And there was him, of course.

He opted to stay night after night—holding her if he could in her bed, or making due with the reclining chair in the corner—more than he didn't.

"It wasn't about me," Vaslav informed, likely the most information Demyan had been able to gather since the bomb blew. "So it had practically nothing to do with her."

"Someone put a bomb at her house! And you really think—"

"There's no need to yell, but I honestly don't have the patience for it, either. I could hang up, except this is a prime opportunity for the two of us."

"For *what?*" Demyan barked.

"To inform you. I'm sending Vera to spend the rest of the winter with you and her mother, stateside. Shouldn't that make you happy—or is the job too hard for you, Demyan?"

The revelation gained him two drastically different reactions from Demyan and his daughter.

"Absolutely *not*," Vera snapped.

Demyan, on the other hand, only asked, "Are you getting the flight plans together, or should I?"

"I'll leave that to you."

"Fine by me—get my daughter's walking papers."

Vaslav sighed, but the woman across the room hadn't taken her eyes off him for a second. "She's not particularly happy about it."

"I'm *not* going to the states for the winter."

From her hospital bed, dressed in a standard gray medical gown—with a second that she wore turned around as a cape around her shoulders—Vera stared Vaslav down like she was daring him to tell her differently. He hated to be the bearer of bad news, but they simply didn't have another choice.

This was for the best.

The further she was from Russia, the more damage he could do to any and everyone who might have put her in this fucking hospital in the first place.

"Oh well for her," Demyan returned.

Silently, Vaslav thought: *touché.*

He wasn't foolish enough to actually say it. Even that didn't last long before her gaze drifted away to the stiff blankets tucked in tight around her on the bed. It was her quiet moments lately that killed him the most because that's when he saw the sadness she couldn't hide in her eyes.

Even if she wasn't crying.

Even if there weren't tears.

Inside, in her heart, he knew she hurt. It constantly radiated from her every second that he was in her presence whether they were talking, and she was smiling, or not. An ever-present cloud hanging over the two of them that she, for some reason, wouldn't speak about.

He tried to understand. They'd had something just long enough to have it ripped away. Before they could be happy or angry; before a single decision about her pregnancy was even considered between them, the selfishness of someone else made the call.

So, he tried. To give her time. For her to be quiet. *If that's what she needs*, he thought. Yet nothing, not even her, suggested what he did was helping.

"Tell my daughter that I love her, and her mother and I will see her soon," Demyan said before he abruptly ended the phone call.

Vaslav didn't take offense, and tossed the device to the middle of Vera's bed where she could grab it if she wanted. Not that she did once she seen the screen was black again.

"You *are* going across the pond," he told her before she could argue.

"Hannah's—"

"Still not awake, *kisska*. And considering it's been two weeks, and they still won't let you into her ICU room … I don't know what you want me to say."

Vera's shoulders dropped with her hard exhale. "She's not dead just because she's in a coma."

"I didn't say that, either."

"She's not even brain dead."

"Vera—"

"Who is she gonna wake up to if you make me go?" she asked. "Hannah shouldn't wake up alone."

He didn't correct her.

That was still a *what if*.

Vaslav's silence said more than he could, anyway. His wife blinked, and wet tears spilled down her cheeks instantly. The droplets clung to her lashes just long enough for him to see them drop, and down with them went what remained of his sad, broken heart.

Fuck him for even having one.

"You'll be better in New York," he said. "Safer."

He needed time to work. Igor required time to heal. It was obvious why Vera would be better off in a place farther away from him and danger while those things happened.

Everything took time; something already too precious, and lacking in Vaslav's life. The irony of it wasn't lost on him.

"I don't want to send you away, either," he told Vera, shrugging under the heavy weight of his parka that he hadn't even taken off after entering the hospital. Just before visiting hours were officially over and security locked the private halls.

Kiril took the Hummer to Dubna.

It—and the teen—would be back in the parking lot by tomorrow morning.

Vera's hands slapped her thighs overtop the blankets, but there wasn't much more fight in her. She even winced.

Compliments of her three broken ribs.

And one punctured lung.

That was before the bump on the back of her head, all the other scrapes and bruises, and the heartbeat of a baby that couldn't be found. Some of the surface things were easier to fix than what couldn't be seen.

Strange how that worked.

"I wish you'd tell me what's wrong," he said, then. "How I could fix that way you keep looking at me—always *sad*."

He was a coward.

Vaslav wouldn't deny it now.

He couldn't ask her what he really wondered. Did she look at him that way because he'd not been happy about a baby that in the end, didn't even get a chance to exist? Did she think she couldn't be sad because she thought he wasn't, either?

"Anything," he told her. "Tell me anything to fix it, and I will."

Vera's shoulders lifted with an almost silent sob, but the noisy wet sound echoed in the quiet room nonetheless. "I don't know, Vas. I just ... I just don't know."

The undertones of sadness clinging to her every word made him flinch, and he fought the urge to put distance between him and her emotions. Instead, he went to her. Arms opened wide if she would let him hold her, and she *did*.

"I'm still trying to figure out how I feel," she mumbled against his chest while her hands fisted handfuls of his jacket to keep him close to her. "And now you're just shipping me off. We're barely newlyweds, that's not fair. Who says *you're* well enough to be—"

"Let's not go there," he interjected.

Vera didn't push the line.

Ignoring the pressure that had been constant and worsening inside his skull—for most of the fucking week—Vaslav nuzzled the top of Vera's head, and dotted kisses along her forehead. It was easier to pretend like his head wasn't splitting open when all of his time and energy needed to be focused on her. Then he swept away the stray strands of dark, silky hair framing her face as she stared up at him.

"I wanted to be able to figure it out at home." she said, lips quivering and tears still welling. "*With you*."

He pressed a soft kiss to her frowning mouth.

"I'm sorry, Vera."

Vaslav meant what he said, and sending her away

wouldn't help him, certainly, but knew his apology would mean very little. In the end, she was still going to New York. Nobody said she had to like it.

"It won't be for long," he added.

A lie he hoped she would willingly cling to. Vaslav had no idea how long cleaning this mess would take.

17.

Three months later ...

"Ma thinks you're depressed."

"Ma also thinks the neighbors try to spy on her, and that you use drugs," Vera returned as an attempt to shut her younger brother up.

Shocker.

It didn't work. Very little did when it came to Roman Avdonin.

"The neighbors *do* spy on them—they're exhibitionists—and everybody knows I have a taste for coke, Vera. Get with the program. Nobody says it to my face."

Vera's brow shot high. The most expression her brother's one-sided conversation had gained from her since he had joined her on the rear patio made of grey stones. Surrounding an in-ground pool that wouldn't be opened and filled until the end of the month— May came faster than she expected it to—the patio extended ten feet around the coping edge on all sides. With tall, thick green hedges partitioning off a section of the backyard to make it feel cozier, she found it just allowed her some quiet time.

She tossed a glance her brother's way, thinking only *usually*.

Bouncing his knees, and tapping his palms to his thighs with a fast beat, Roman couldn't sit still on his chair. Not even when Vera kept staring at him.

"What?" Roman asked when he noticed his older sister's look.

"Which ones are the exhibitionists—Ma and Papa, or the neighbors?"

He barked a laugh. "You'll figure it out."

Lord.

Vera had only been half joking.

Roman, who had come to sit with her outside in the backyard without any explanation, gave a good, hard sniff as he leaned the chair back dangerously on two legs.

"The coke will kill you," Vera said.

He rocked with the chair like his whole body was nodding in agreement with Vera's warning, but the way he smirked a little and his jaw worked like it was chewing on words said he probably didn't care.

His next words confirmed it.

"Yeah, maybe that's what I'm going for," Roman said.

Vera just rolled her eyes.

Even when it came to his substance abuse, her brother didn't have the patience or give-a-damn to listen if someone wasn't saying what he wanted to hear. Every human had their flaws; Roman rarely tried to hide his.

"And Ma does, by the way," he tacked on at the end with extra attitude. "Think you're depressed, I mean."

His defensiveness about their mother said he was telling the truth about her concerns, but it was the least of Vera's, honestly. She didn't know how to break that news to Roman.

"It's all I hear her talk about every night when she calls," her brother added the longer Vera remained silent across the pool. "Which means she's talked herself out with Papa, and now she's moved to *me*. And no matter how many times I tell her that you're a grown ass woman who can be as sad as she wants about whatever she wants—"

"She's not wrong," Vera interrupted before Roman could rant on further.

His bright blue gaze—the same as hers—narrowed.

Vera shrugged. "I *am* depressed. I just don't want to talk about it."

That should be simple enough for anyone to understand, even Roman, who on his best days, didn't often think of those around him. Selfish to an extreme, her wild younger brother lived life on the edge constantly. That left little time or space for the thoughts and feelings of others. Not that she blamed him for being that way, really.

"Because you're not in Russia?" he asked after a moment.

Vera sighed.

If only it was that easy ...

"Because I'm not in Russia," she agreed, then adding just as quickly, "or because my husband calls once a week, and tells me exactly nothing. I mentioned earlier how my villa was ruined by a bomb, didn't I? Years of life just … gone."

Every photo.

The plants.

Vera still felt like the bomb had happened so quickly, and because she had not yet been back to Noble Row, it was still surreal in her mind. Not entirely *real*. She couldn't picture it; couldn't wrap her mind around what she was told would now be her reality. How was this big part of her history just gone?

She knew it was.

Maybe she just had to *see* it.

But that was only one problem.

Bigger ones awaited.

"Or it could be because my best friend is still in a coma, and her mother's been actively working to abort her fetus but there's not a thing I can do," Vera added, gesturing broadly in front of herself.

Well, she couldn't do much but the circumstances and a few phone calls by Vaslav might have helped to move some things along. The only thing her husband would entertain with conversation when pressed by Vera beyond the weather in his part of the world, but she gave Vaslav credit. He had made every effort he could to help.

It did.

Hannah's circumstance worked to her favor, too. Significant brain activity and a letter from Hannah's physician who had privately confirmed the pregnancy with her initially had put a momentary halt in her mother's plans. Hannah had wanted her child, and her body was capable of carrying the baby to term. Or damn close to it.

Marlena Malone wouldn't get her way.

Vera was working just as hard as the bitch to make

sure of it.

"Life's a little messy," Roman muttered.

Vera scoffed. "Nice way to put it."

"Yeah, well …"

He didn't even bother to finish his sentence, what good would it do? As it was, Vera had already figured out her brother's reason for seeking their parents home out on the outskirts of the city while the sky burned brightly with the colors of the sunset.

"What, are you worried about me, too?"

Roman snorted, and folded his tattooed arms over his broad, muscular chest. His gaze remained fixated on the edge of the blue tile along the edge of the pool instead of her as he replied, "Get real—I'm not patting your head and telling you everything's gonna be okay. That's Ma's job, Vera."

"Doesn't matter, anyway. Wouldn't help if you did."

He met her gaze then.

Vera offered him a sad smile, muttering, "Nothing's okay, so."

Roman exhaled the breath he'd been holding, replying dully, "*Yeah*. I hate when shit feels like that. Makes everything else worse."

A human condition. Or that's how her husband would have explained it away.

The quiet stillness between Vera and her brother at least felt comforting to her, but she wouldn't bother to tell Roman as much. He wasn't the type for deep feelings and introspective conversations that dug beyond surface level things. A lot like their father, in that way, he found it easier to deal with the tougher shit when he wasn't breaking to pieces over it.

She still loved her brother, though.

Adored him for sitting quietly with her while the sun sat around them, and the early May evening air crept in with a chilliness that made her grateful she had pulled on a thick hoodie.

"She doesn't know, either," Vera said under her breath. "So all Ma's got to go on about me is what she sees and does know. Which isn't much."

The top of the edge at her brother's back became the focal point for her attention as she kept her tone level and her thoughts blank. It was easier that way because then she didn't fall into a puddle of her own tears.

"Know what?" Roman asked.

Right.

She hadn't explained that bit.

"The day the bomb went off in front of my villa, I found out I was pregnant that morning," Vera said, shrugging one shoulder like it wouldn't make that news a big deal. She didn't want it to be something that her brother made a spectacle out of, even if it was just to apologize to her when she delivered the next part of the story. "And then I woke up three days later in the hospital with no baby inside me."

Vera laughed a bleak sound, but nothing about this was very funny. It just made everything easier to swallow. "I passed everything before I could even take a second to love what was there before it wasn't. It's kind of weird. I'm not sure how you grieve something you didn't have. So all I want is to go back to the place I was before this happened. Happy with my new husband. Do you know what I mean?"

Roman had turned into stone across the pool. "No, I can't say that I do, but I'm a dude without a uterus. The only thing I think about when babies come to my mind is stabbing myself in the eye."

"Nice, Rome."

Another man in her life who didn't sugarcoat shit. It really was no big shocker why Vera gravitated toward a husband like the one she now had when someone took a good look at the rest of the men she loved in one way or another.

Her brother grunted something unintelligible under his breath. It might have been an apology, or something else, but Vera wasn't looking for that sort of sympathy.

He waved a hand while his other stroked his chin and down his jaw. "My point was—okay—that no, I can't imagine how you feel, and it sucks you gotta feel that way at all right now."

Raking her fingers through her hair—left loose and cut into an angular bob yet again—as she leaned back on the lawn chair, she continued using her fingertips to massage her scalp, across her cheekbones, and then at her temples. She wished it would help with the way even her face felt exhausted.

As if that was a real thing.

Except it seemed to be.

For her. Every part of her was tired. Of everything. Even moving and being. Something else about depression that nobody talked about—it wasn't just being *sad*. There was so much more to the empty loneliness, a constantly growing hole, someone felt even when standing in a room full of people they loved. Or how getting out of bed every day was a chore, and only to be done when needed.

Cleaning?

What the fuck was that?

So had been Vera's life in a nutshell for the past

months that she'd been staying with her parents in New York. Day after day. Night after night. The same thing, it never changed. Yes, she was absolutely sad, but it was so much more than that, too.

No wonder her ma noticed. Claire probably knew she also couldn't fix it, but making others around Vera aware of her situation at least offered her kindness, love, and support. For that, she was grateful.

Eventually, Roman decided to restart the conversation when he popped his tongue off the roof of his mouth. "So, I have a question. If you don't mind."

"Since when did my little brother ever care if I minded about something?"

His chest heaved with a gusty breath. "Dad told me after he came home from Russia that you seemed less prone to bullshit. I kind of took it as a fair warning."

Huh.

"What was your question?" Vera asked.

All the arrogance that made up her brother's personality had bled away the longer they sat together outside. He actually looked more like his twenty-one years sitting across from her—young and foolish about it. She missed being like that.

Carefree.

"So how come I know about the pregnancy thing," Roman asked, "but Ma doesn't? I mean, it's *Ma*, Vera. I don't particularly like to be mothered, but we both know she's good at what she does. Maybe you need it, huh? Why not tell her? At least, she's someone to talk to. Me, I just—fuck," he swore, gesturing at his distressed acid wash jeans with the blown out knees, combat boots laced high on his feet, and the leather jacket he'd thrown over a plain black shirt. "Look at me. We both know I'm not here to do any feelings."

"I don't want to tell everybody," she replied," but I needed to tell *somebody*."

Not even Hannah was there to listen.

Not right now.

"Maybe I thought my annoying little brother was the best person to share a secret with," she added. "I wasn't asking for you to cry with me. Just for you to keep your promise."

Roman smiled, but it wasn't very wide. "I *did* pinky promise to keep all your secrets once, didn't I?"

She never let him forget it when given the chance. Like now.

"You were six, and *really* wanted that extra brownie."

As a girl, she'd had no trouble at all manipulating her little brother. Frankly, her kid brother had made it easy.

He all out grinned at the mention of his favorite treat. Some things never changed. "Still do—I'd kill for one of Ma's brownies right now."

"I could make that happen," Vera offered.

The excited anticipation that had her brother leaping forward in his chair made her laugh. And smile, too. Both things that she hadn't been doing very much of lately.

"Tell me how," Roman demanded.

Vera nodded to the side, directing Roman's attention to the row of ten two-gallon pots of Hydrangeas that Claire had brought home from a nearby nursery. A variety of blooms, her mother's backyard would have a rainbow of colorful flowers from June through September.

"Those," she said.

"What about them? Ma said she got those for you."

Claire had.

A tactic to draw Vera out of her room, really. It worked but only because Claire was not the gardening type. She enjoyed gardens that were well-maintained and ready to pick or prune. Less when it came to the grunt work of actually putting things in the ground.

That was work *Vera* liked.

"I need some holes dug," she told her brother.

"Today?"

"It's better to plant them at night."

Roman sucked air through his teeth. "Are the brownies already cooked?"

"Nope, but I bet I could get Ma started in less than ten minutes."

He rubbed his hands together, pleased. "And they'll be done by the time I finish the holes."

"Exactly."

"Deal," Roman muttered. "Where's Dad's shovel?"

Vera laughed again as she pushed up from the chair, heading for the sliding glass doors leading into the rear of the house. "I'm sure you'll find it. Don't start before I've marked the holes, Roman."

He waved two fingers dismissively over his shoulder. "Yeah, yeah."

"I'm serious." Vera stopped at the doors, pausing before pulling them open so she could privately tell her brother, "And thanks. For listening, you know?"

Roman glanced back at her from over his shoulder. "No problem. I still think it might help to share that secret with somebody else, though. You've got a lot to deal with. It's okay to just say so."

Was it?

Was the hurricane that had become her life as a newlywed just a lot to deal with? Did phrasing it exactly like that encompass the overwhelming anxiety that crippled her some days? Vera didn't think so, and she couldn't say she knew how to start to fix it, either. Or if she even wanted to.

Well.

Actually, she did.

"I'd really just like to go home," she told Roman. "I'm happy when I'm there; I can deal with everything—anything—there. Instead, I'm stuck here."

Without Vas, she opted not to add out loud.

Roman nodded, but his silence at the mention of her returning to Russia said more than he would to her face with literal words. Like her father, her brother believed that her marriage to Vaslav meant they were no longer allowed to make certain calls with Vera. Even if it was something like talking about her husband's current situation in his motherland.

If Vaslav had nothing to say, then neither did they.

The not knowing didn't make things better. Not when she woke up every morning feeling like she had already lost something precious and was on the verge of losing someone else. If anything, being kept in the dark was killing her.

"For what it's worth," her brother said as Vera reached for the sliding door's handle, "I'm sorry— you know, that you hurt right now. For any reason. I wish you didn't hurt."

"Yeah, me too." Vera blinked away the tears she'd managed to keep to the privacy of her bed and evening showers. "You were right—this life's fucking messy."

18.

"Did you get all your mother's hydrangeas planted?"

"Have *you* started to plant the juvenile beauties yet?" Vera returned, referring to the lilacs in terracotta pots that he'd just checked over that morning before leaving the house.

"I promised I wouldn't without you," Vaslav said. "And my question wasn't about me, *kisska*."

"I want to come home, Vaslav."

"*Da*, yes, I know."

The silence on the other end of the call extended both ways. He offered his young wife nothing else except he acknowledged her wants and feelings, and in kind, she gave him back exactly the same. *Nothing*.

A lot of their conversations had gone this unfortunate way since her departure to New York. At first, she'd been more than willing to spend hours on the phone discussing everything and anything she could pull out of him, in between begging for him to let her come home. It seemed like now she had diverted to a new path to make Vaslav suffer for his choices.

She wouldn't even talk to him.

Not unless required.

"Vera, listen to me—"

"Cut the shit. You know it just makes me more bitter, right?" she asked him then before letting out a weak laugh. "I hate even saying that. Admitting it. I love you, but you're making it really hard for me to do that right now."

"There are but a few reasons you want to be in Moscow right now, Vera."

"*And?*"

"And not one of them will be fixed or better because you are here," he said, internally willing it to be the last word he had to make on the topic.

Vaslav wasn't stupid.

He knew it wouldn't be the last.

It didn't matter how true his statement was—or that he could list off every reason she would point to for her need to return and rebuke it with an equally valid reason to say no. She would stay where she was until he considered Russia safe for her to return. There would be no more bombs catching her in the crossfire, or anyone else around her, for that matter.

Things like that took time.

"Fine, Vaslav," Vera muttered heavily, defeat coloring up her tone. "Do whatever you want—I guess, call me when it's done? Whatever the hell it is you're doing day after day without me."

Nothing good, he wanted to tell her but he didn't. *Nothing half as amazing as what I could be doing at home with you*, he could have said, and it would have been the truth.

He also wished for that to be true, but just because he wanted his wife home with him didn't mean he could allow his feelings to cloud his judgement about what happened in the first place. There was a reason why he sent Vera to New York, and he didn't intend on bringing her back before he made sure that reason never happened again.

It wasn't his fault that she couldn't see this situation from his perspective. Vaslav was to blame for a lot of things, but not that one.

"Could you at least say hi to Hannah for me?" she asked, referencing the only reason he was able to keep her on the phone call for more than a cursory hi and bye. As had happened for their last three conversations after she answered, asked him if he was calling to let her know she could come home, and after he refused, she would simply hang up.

"Otherwise," Vera continued, "just fuck off."

Her cold dismissal came with the click of her phone, and then soon after, a dial tone. Interestingly enough, that was the same moment his elevator reached the intended floor he had selected at the beginning of his call. Just as Vera had first picked up the call.

He was left listening to the emptiness on the other end of the line, still hearing Vera's final *fuck you* eating its way through his tired brain, and staring at his warped reflection in the widening door panels of the elevator. He stood there long enough after the doors had slid entirely open that they started to close again.

Vera's anger was justified, too.

He had to keep reminding himself that.

Vaslav needed the closing doors as a wakeup call to

remind him what he was there to do. Stepping into the dimly lit corridor, Vaslav followed the signs and arrows to the long-term ICU ward where Hannah Malone had been kept from the moment Bogdan Nikitin agreed to take her file onto his team's caseload. As his patient, he made the final calls on everything from the state of her fetus, medications and therapies, and even transportation.

Say, flying the comatose woman back to her mother in Italy where Marlena could get Hannah a new doctor that would do whatever her mother wanted.

Something the young woman's mother had recently tried to use to her benefit, not that it worked. Marlena could cry foul all she wanted; it wouldn't do any good. Unless she came to Moscow to sit in Bogdan's office for a review of her daughter's coma and the prognosis, nobody planned to entertain anything from her.

Or so said Vaslav's current payroll.

Money really was the only talking point when it came to a situation like this. He had more than enough to make sure he sat at the very head of the table, having his voice heard first. Nobody else but the people he paid needed to know that he was speaking, however.

This wasn't his first trip on the ride of manipulating someone's future without them being aware he was doing it. Although, in the past, he'd never done it with the intention to keep someone else alive. That bit was new. He typically went for the opposite route.

There were some pros to keeping one's friends close. Like Bogdan. Not that Vaslav needed many more friends. *Any*more, really. As it was, the friends he had seemed to take a lot of his energy. Something he didn't have much of, frankly; just getting up every day took most of it.

"Mr. Pashkov, did you forget your visitor badge again?" the familiar woman behind the nurse's station asked. She offered him a kind, patient smile even as he scowled at her on his way by the desk. "You know what happens when the security asks you for it, that's all I'm saying."

Her voice—Alyona, was her name—carried behind him even though she barely raised her voice. One didn't need to be loud in the ICU ward to be heard. It was something he made an effort to keep in the back of his mind whenever he came for a visit. He didn't need anyone overhearing his conversations with Bogdan, but as this was the only place that the man would really entertain a visit from Vaslav, well …

He had no choice.

It worked out.

Hannah needed someone to stop by and say hello.

"Yeah, yeah," Vaslav told the head nurse with a wave over his shoulder when she called his name one more time. He didn't bother with their attempts at conversation. Any of the nurses, really. Bogdan requested it; Vaslav had no issue making himself appear unapproachable when needed.

The nurse didn't have the opportunity to say anything else before Vaslav headed through the automatic sliding glass doors that opened to room *202*. As soon as he crossed the threshold of the temperature-controlled room filled with screens monitoring every inch of Hannah's prone, sheet-covered body on the reclined hospital bed, the doors slid shut with a hiss behind him.

The first time he'd been there—he almost didn't walk through those doors. In fact, he stared at the numbers over the doors for entirely too long overthinking whether or not the young woman on the other side would care or want him there.

Bogdan had shown up and made the choice for Vaslav that day when he hadn't been willing to explain why the thought of going inside the room bothered him.

Surprisingly, Bogdan wasn't the man waiting for him on the one of two chairs that sat side by side in the farthest left corner of Hannah's room.

"Finally decided to show up, did you?" Vaslav asked.

A sigh passed Igor's scarred lips, and while he'd looked Vaslav's way when he first arrived, now the man only stared at the unmoving woman on the bed. "Bogdan got a page. He'll be around in a—"

"Yeah, yeah. Back to you."

Igor's dark eyes followed Vaslav across the room until he had joined the man in the empty chair next to his. "What about me?"

"I said it. You're here. Many moons later, mind you, but—"

"Thank you, Captain Obvious."

Igor even had the audacity to smile. Except it was more like a wincing sneer. Vaslav didn't bother to smile back, and instead, put his focus on shedding his heavy tweed coat. Next to him, his companion—the only one conscious and talking—remained silent and had gone back to staring in the general vicinity of the bed.

One couldn't tell when Igor had a coat on, buttoned up to the neck, but a good sixty percent of his chest, back, and legs had been burned in the bomb made of screws of shrapnel and some type of petrol for fuel. Igor had only taken a few flying pieces of metal to his face and neck. All injuries that had healed rather quickly.

The burns, on the other hand …

The fact the man was even up and walking around spoke to a miracle. He should still be deep within the walls of a burn unit, but a nurse on his twenty-four-hour call at home—or rather, his current safehouse—allowed the man more privacy.

"Are you going back for another surgery?" Vaslav asked.

The eight-hour skin-grafting procedure Igor had done the month before had only been partially successful. As far as Vaslav knew. Igor didn't like to get detailed about his current struggles, and Vaslav wasn't the type to prod.

Igor swallowed audibly, letting out a shaky breath. "They said it might help to get another graft on my back, but at this point, I'm running out of usable skin."

"I hear donor—"

"Not interested. They already put some fucking fish scales on me when I was in there the first time. Jesus Christ."

Vaslav cringed, but didn't question Igor on the topic further. There were some things that men should simply be able to keep to themselves. Undignified—or radical, depending on how someone wanted to look at it—medical procedures were certainly one of those things.

"I'm here because Bogdan called," Igor admitted.

"Oh?"

Igor shrugged, his gaze sweeping the many monitors on the wall across from theirs. Unless the nurses were in the room, most of the machines and devices were kept silent for the most part. Occasionally, one thing or another would beep, and shortly thereafter, a nurse would enter the room to do something with the IV pole, a lead on Hannah, or whatever else needed their attention.

Someone kept the young woman's wild, red curls brushed, her lips moist, and the faint hint of vanilla in the air matched the body lotion on the rolling stand next to the bed. The one gash that had been on her face, just above the line of her eyebrow, had been fixed by a plastic surgeon who owed Bogdan a favor. One would need to be studying Hannah's lax features very carefully to see the way the surgeon had stitched the scar along her brow line.

"Do you think she can hear us?" Igor asked.

"She's not dead."

"I know that!"

Vaslav cocked a brow at the slight shout, but he tried to give Igor some grace for it all the same. "I *meant*, she's shown responses to some stimuli. Or her brain activity suggests she had responses. There's research that shows her coma state is similar to others who woke up and proclaimed to have been somewhat lucid or conscious at different times. Can she hear us? It's possible."

Between the three people who had been in the villa the morning the bomb blew, Hannah had been the one with the least visible injuries. Perhaps because she had closed the front door just in time and that blocked her from the initial blast, or it could have just been circumstance. Right place, right time.

Except nothing about this was very right.

Igor shifted subtly on the chair, flinching as he did so and letting out a short gasp of breath that spoke of his pain. An agony he otherwise kept quiet. "Bogdan … he, uh—"

"What?"

"He called me."

Ah.

Vaslav followed Igor's gaze to the woman on the bed, but this time, his friend's stare lingered on Hannah's slightly swollen stomach under the stark white hospital sheet.

"He said an amnio would confirm—probably don't need it, but anyway, getting me listed as the biological father would go a long way to ending the legal matter with Hannah's mother."

"And then what?" Vaslav questioned.

"Pardon?"

"Are you raising the baby? I heard they did an ultrasound last week. Congrats, it's a girl."

Igor turned to him, blinking once, and then twice, slowly. "She could wake up before—"

"At this moment, given what we've got to go on, let's say that she doesn't wake up before they have to take the kid out of her. What are you going to do then?"

"Vaslav, I'm not in the fucking mood today to do this with you, or anyone else. Okay? You're goddamn lucky that I'm even here in this hospital right now."

He wouldn't deny Igor that.

"Let Bogdan do the amnio," Vaslav said. "We can figure out the rest later."

Igor flinched at the comment. "It was just fun. Even that last night—that's why I went there. She took my mind off the rest. I don't get it."

"That makes two of us who are currently confused."

"No, *fuck* ..." Igor pinched at the bridge of his nose, muttering, "She said that was the last time as I was leaving. I understood, you know? Shit ends. There didn't have to be a reason. We weren't a thing, and I didn't even have the time to be messing around with her as it was."

Right.

And clearly, Igor paid the price for that mistake. As every man in their life and position did in one way or another. It was an unfortunate lesson to learn, but Vaslav doubted Igor would allow himself to get so distracted with the personal side of his life that he overlooked the business part that always stayed close behind.

In all their many phone conversations since Igor had felt up to doing so, and more recently, during their plans to handle the bomb situation and the person who planted it, not once had Igor talked about that morning. Not why he was at the villa, although Vaslav had previously thought the reasons were clear, or anything else.

"You didn't even know she was pregnant, did you?" Vaslav asked.

Igor glanced sideways, shrugging. "I'm starting to think she didn't want me to know."

Huh.

Vaslav fixated on the woman in the bed again, wondering how true Igor's statement might be—or whether it even mattered. "As it were, she wanted it," he said, earning himself another wince from Igor. "Vera's sure of that."

"The coma isn't affecting the baby?"

"Her brain is regulating everything that it's supposed to. She hasn't even been on a ventilator for a month," Vaslav explained, folding his arms over his chest. "These are all good signs, or so that fucking idiot upstairs with the big office says. Where is Bogdan, anyway?"

"I told you, he had a page."

Vaslav massaged his pounding head. "Right, right."

"It bothers me."

"That she didn't tell you she was pregnant?"

He really knew better than to assume.

Igor grunted a low *no*, adding louder, "That we haven't figured out who set the bomb."

"Me, too," Vaslav admitted.

Yet, probably not for the same reason. It's what made his wife's worsening phone calls far harder to deal with and get through. He wasn't being entirely forthcoming with Vera about the happenings in Moscow because there was very little to tell.

"But it definitely came from within the brotherhood," Igor muttered. "I was too new into the seat for it to be anyone else. Word hadn't even properly traveled out of the country that a change in leadership had happened."

Vaslav had another thought, then. One he'd wished he could have had earlier. Many months ago, even.

"Did you even get your dues?" he asked, referring to the money that should be handed down from every vor to their boss. At least monthly, the tradition continued on. It guaranteed protection to the man paying, and if accepted by the boss, the payment also promised continued status and permission to keep territory where said man worked.

A delicate balance.

For years, Vaslav just made Nico or Igor collect his money. He stopped doing his official rounds back when he also wanted to stop seeing people. It wasn't like any vor in the country complained. With Vaslav, people tended to go with the flow.

"It should have been the next week," Igor said. "I've put it off—the obvious reason."

Like pain.

And safety.

"Change of plans," Vaslav said suddenly, rising from his chair. Igor didn't follow.

"What plans, Vas?"

"Yours." He turned, and pointed at Igor, saying, "Whoever's running messages for you—send one. Let any man in the bratva know the boss is ready to collect his dues. If we can't find the snake in the grass because there's so many, well, then let's put them into a barrel."

Igor's brow crinkled. "What good is getting them all together going to do?"

"Well, then you can play a game."

"*What* game?" Igor snapped.

Nobody had any patience anymore.

"Eeny, meeny, miny, moe," Vaslav said.

But they wouldn't be catching tigers. Some people *might* lose some toes. Vaslav still had to work out the details.

"Do it the right way," Vaslav told his friend, "and you won't have to worry about another bomb situation again."

At least now, Igor looked slightly more interested. "Tell me how."

19.

"I told your father we'll have to make a trip next year to see it."

"*Maybe*," came the sleepy reply in the background of the phone call. Otherwise, Demyan had remained mostly quiet. "I can't just go to Moscow—there are other people there who might have something to say about that, Claire."

"*I* could make the trip. Who will say something, then?"

"Funny of you to think you'll make any trips without me."

"Don't start with that, Demyan. We know how it goes."

Vera, who hadn't entirely been engaged and listening along well with her mother's attempt at conversation, decided to step in between her parents' shared barbs to ask, "What did you want to see?"

A sigh answered that.

"I thought you'd be happier because you're home,

but you still sound distracted and sad," Claire eventually said.

"I'm not home yet."

Almost.

Claire didn't argue the point, instead telling her stepdaughter, "Spring, Vera. I was saying how beautiful Russia must be in the spring. It'd be nice to see it firsthand. *Next year*, even."

Right, right.

"And then your father had to go ahead and get his opinion in before anyone even bothered to ask him for it," Claire added.

Although, it didn't sound like the comment had been meant specifically for Vera. Demyan also picked up on that fact when he muttered in reply, "Quit looking at me like that, *dushka*."

"You don't know that I'm looking at you, Demyan."

"I can feel your eyes on my back, Claire."

As nice—or not—as this conversation was, Vera had to be honest and admit that she just wasn't into it. Usually her parents' banter made her smile, but the anxious anticipation that had thickened in her chest with every mile that closed between her and Vaslav now took up most of her attention. She couldn't even breathe around it anymore.

It wasn't Demyan and Claire's fault.

It wasn't even Vera's.

Except the man who was the cause wouldn't apologize for his part, and she had yet to decide how to deal with that fact. Some things really did take time. At least, love allowed her the grace of patience to do so.

Or try, anyhow.

"Listen," she said to her mother, still picking off the remnants of her last French manicure because she needed *something* to do other than stare out of the windows of her current ride, "I'll try to call you back later. Maybe tomorrow, but I wanted to visit Hannah, so—"

"Ma'am," interjected the driver behind the wheel of the town car, "did you say the gate would be open or closed when we arrived?"

"I'll let you go," Claire said, having not heard Vera's driver quietly announce their arrival to the Dubna estate.

Vera, who had gone as far as calling her mother knowing there were only minutes to spare before she'd finally be home, managed to distract herself from a panic attack by doing so. Yet, she'd also forgotten how close she was to the house.

But there it was.

Looming at the top of the hill, the colonial seemed to stare Vera down from its higher position. What little snow remained only served to leave small slushy banks at the end of the driveway, but even the grass had started to pop green in places. Overhead, the bright afternoon sky scattered with fluffy white clouds seemed to stretch on forever and ever beyond the hills.

More interesting were the beauties.

Both adult lilacs at the gate were in full bloom with large white blossoms she could practically smell through the windows of the car. She almost wished that she had a pair of shears to take a few cuttings up to the house, but maybe someone else had already done so.

If not, that was the very first thing she planned to

do.

"Ma," Vera said quietly.

Even though she hadn't responded yet to her driver.

"Yeah, Vera?"

"You're right—Russia is beautiful in the spring. It's a great time to come."

Claire took more than a few seconds to reply, but the murmurings on the other end of the call said her mother had relayed the information to Demyan, as well. "We'll have to figure something out, won't we?"

"Yeah, sure."

"Give Vas my love," Claire said.

"I will."

Once Vera had ended the call, she found the driver's expectant gaze searching for hers in the rearview mirror. "Ma'am?"

"It's Vera."

The man, who wore a standard black suit as a uniform, and topped it off with black leather gloves and a cap with his employer's logo on the front, smiled thinly.

"Mrs. Pashkov, is the gate supposed to be opened or closed?"

She gave him some credit when he didn't call her a ma'am for the third time, but he remained as formal as he possibly could without being rude all the same.

So was life.

A give and take.

"It's unlocked," she said, offering nothing else.

Actually, before he could reply, Vera had already unbuckled her seatbelt and opened the rear passenger door. The man rushed to do the same, and join her, but as his door swung open, she waved a hand at him, and rolled her eyes.

"Relax, I'm just opening the gate," she told him.

He remained frozen half in and out of the car with one hand on the top of the opened door, watching as Vera unlatched the heavy iron gate that had been repainted a bright white recently. There were still paint splatters on the ground, but the white on the metal had been dry.

With both Beauty of Moscows hugging either side of the gate attached to stone and mortal pillars, the new paint made it stand out even more against the backdrop of the property it was meant to protect. For some reason, the color made it seem less threatening to Vera's eye and more welcoming. She didn't know if that had been Vaslav's reasoning for whipping out the paint and brush, or if he just meant to give Vera something new to see when she arrived home.

It was a nice change.

Not that it made up for anything.

As she shoved it open, letting the weight swing the gate without much effort on her part at all, the driver said, "Ah, so that's what you meant. I'll remember it next time—promise."

Vera laughed. Mostly to herself, but she didn't hide it.

Her driver wouldn't understand the joke, so she didn't bother to explain her amusement at his inquisitive look. They never had the same driver twice. Something else Vaslav paid good money for when it came to the car services he liked to use. It was also a requirement he demanded the service follow through on. He'd already dropped two companies for making the mistake.

"I'm going to walk up from here," Vera told the

driver.

"I was told to drop you off at the house and—"

"I will walk up from here," she repeated.

Her tone did the job.

The man shrugged, and let go of the door as he dropped back inside the vehicle. Before he could slam the door shut, Vera called, "You don't have to wait up there for me. Just drop the bags off at the steps. It's fine."

Not that Vaslav would think so.

Too bad for him.

Vera waited as the car slipped beyond the gate before she started her trek up the hill. Only a slight chill in the breeze kept her extra alert as she took a moment to admire the tall beauties with their beautiful blooms.

Beyond the adult lilacs, the few juveniles Vaslav had planted on either side of the driveway also had blooms and even new growth that Vera could distinguish from how the plants had looked when she came to the property the previous June.

She didn't bother to close the gate behind her.

Something caught her attention instead.

A dozen terracotta pots, six on either side, lined the driveway where they had been spaced evenly apart all the way up. Every beauty that had sat in front of the house, the ones Vaslav had promised to wait to plant until she was home to do it with him, waited for her in the spots he wanted them to go in the ground.

She didn't stop at each one.

Only a couple.

Here and there ...

The time it took for her to look over the plants gave her more to think, and breathe. She wanted that heady, floral scent carrying in the breeze to fill up her lungs and stay there because it helped so much with that anxiety in her chest. So much so, she could ignore it again as she made her way up the remainder of the winding drive.

Vaslav called her home in much the same way he had sent her away. With little to no warning, without her input, and it left Vera feeling like a vessel in a storm of her husband's making. Thrashed by emotional waves, unsteady on her feet, and not quite settled in her heart. Her complaints were certainly heard, but they had never been corrected, and that made everything else harder.

She explained that to Vaslav, too.

Being home *should* help.

Or that's what Vera kept telling herself.

At the halfway point, the driver waved to her on his way back down to the gate. Three quarters of the way up, with only fifty or so feet left for her to walk before she entered the circular section of the driveway with the towering birch trees in the middle, well, her hands started to shake.

Just a little.

Those nerves came back fast.

Maybe she expected to reach the ridge of the hill and drive to see Vaslav standing at the top of the stairs leading to the front door of the house wearing his familiar scowl while he stared at the bags the driver had left for her to carry up the steps. Except her husband wasn't waiting there for her at all, but the steps weren't completely empty, either.

The sight of a grinning Kiril still made Vera smile.

It could have been the way he lazily waved two fingers in her direction where he sat on the bottom step with his booted feet resting on one of her rolling bags that gained her smile. Really, it was simply the familiar face waiting for her.

It made the place feel more like home even if she hadn't left the place while Kiril was there to see her go, he was still a reminder of her memories here. In a way. She wouldn't deny that it made her happy to find him there with his distressed leather jacket and denim jeans with blown out knees, either.

"Still hiding from Mira outside?" she asked Kiril as she rounded the towering birch trees.

The teenager shrugged. "Not really. Just thought you might need some help with your bags."

"Was today Vaslav's drop-off day, or what?"

Kiril shrugged one shoulder, and then dropped his boots to the ground before pushing up from the step. "Nah, I've been here since the weekend."

"Here," she said.

"*Da*—yeah."

"At the house."

Kiril just stared at her, confused. "I said that?"

He had.

Vera needed a minute to catch up. Apparently, a few things had changed since she left. Someone hadn't filled her in about the changes, so here she was, figuring it all out on her own. Interestingly enough, Vaslav had not mentioned the fact that Kiril was spending more time in Dubna again, let alone at the house. Considering the fit he'd thrown over Kiril, she was more than curious about the slice of humble pie Vaslav had needed to swallow to let the kid in again.

Or did his reason come from somewhere else?

The man of the hour was nowhere to ask.

Surprise.

"Did he at least give you a bedroom?" she asked, folding her arms over her chest.

Kiril nodded. "In Mira's suites. She still babies me a lot." He scoffed then, and made a face. "Well, all the fuckin' time, I mean."

Vera didn't suppress her smile. "But?"

"I never go hungry."

Yeah, she bet.

And he also wasn't alone.

That probably made the rest easier to swallow, but Vera seriously doubted Kiril would appreciate it if she pointed that out. So, she opted not to.

Eyeing the house while Kiril grabbed a handle on each bag of rolling luggage—leaving only a small duffle bag for Vera to carry—her gaze eventually traveled to the front door. A door that remained closed despite her arrival, and a car that had come up the drive and then gone. Something that never happened without Vaslav going to the front door.

Or checking the windows above on the second floor.

Not even the drapes had moved.

The obvious question she could no longer ignore started to slip out of her mouth before she was even ready to ask it. Her heart had a way of doing that to her—controlling her brain.

Vera kind of hated it.

"Where is my husband?"

She should have asked it the second she noticed her blush-white Hummer had been taken from the shed and parked at the far end of the circular drive.

Without its black companion.

Like her, the vehicle was alone.

Kiril cleared his throat, but he didn't avoid her stare when she looked to him for an actual answer. The question hadn't been rhetorical, after all.

"Well?" she demanded. "Don't lie and tell me he's here."

Clearly, he wasn't.

Kiril's lips puckered with consideration, but he let it all go with a noisy sigh. "Probably killing people."

Vera blinked. "*What?*"

His answer seemed ridiculous, but his following silence made her reconsider her initial thought.

Was it?

"Kiril," Vera started.

He only shrugged again. "I'm just saying—he might have gotten mad and wanted you to come home. All I know is he said that to do that, people had to die. You don't ask him questions, Vera. Okay? He says shit like that, and you just don't ask."

Well.

He wasn't wrong.

Vera didn't entirely understand the situation at hand, but the teenager with the apparent answers had moved to other business. Like her luggage.

Kiril pulled the rolling pieces behind him as he climbed the steps. "Oh, and fair warning … the smell of the roses are only a little overwhelming at first. I promise it gets better."

She stared at the back of his retreating head, more confused than ever.

"What roses?"

"The house," he told her, correcting quickly with, "well, the foyer—it's full of them."

That comment had Vera sprinting forward beyond Kiril on the steps to reach the door first.

What else did Vaslav do?
She soon found out.
Kiril hadn't lied.
The house opened to white roses *everywhere*.

20.

The roses weren't the only thing waiting to surprise Vera inside the house. Not once in their many phone conversations had her husband mentioned the fact that he had allowed the contractor who she'd met with before and after the wedding to go ahead with their renovation plans on the first and second floors. She noticed the difference downstairs first because the doors across from Vaslav's den no longer existed and instead, the hallway opened wider into the studio space that now connected to the set of suites upstairs.

She only briefly stopped at the various art easels and stacked, unused canvases, turning a wide circle to take in the tables full of supplies she had mentioned in passing would be nice, and then she headed for the winding metal stars in the very middle of the room.

Every step seemed to chime under her footsteps on the way up. Alone to discover the changes—as Kiril had taken her bags upstairs and Mira yelled her greeting from the kitchen and promised food would be ready soon—Vera tried not to feel guilty about the excitement swelling in her heart as she entered the upstairs suites.

Unlike the open concept studio-like space below, some of the walls that sectioned off the suites upstairs remained standing. Except she hadn't wanted to keep any doors between the different rooms, and the contractor had assured he could condense the many spaces into two larger ones without compromising the integrity of the rest of the house. The stairwell led up to a small alcove where it opened to both rooms with tall windows where the light spilled in to cover nearly every inch. Morning and afternoon light that wouldn't be too harsh for the indoor plants but would keep them growing and thriving all year long.

She didn't expect to find any plants already waiting, some with nursery tags still attached and others in different sized terracotta pots, but it stopped Vera in her tracks. The bigger pots sat on the floor while a couple of small growing vines had been placed on the windowsill with room to hang. A table made of glossy oak sat in the middle of the larger room covered in tools, hangers, pots, and even a high pile of soil that had managed to stay on the table instead of the freshly waxed hardwood floors.

She hadn't even taken the time to look at the other side, with the smaller room, but already Vera could tell … it was perfect.

Every bit of it.

Yes, it still needed some work. She had planned for shelves but wanted Vaslav to build them once she picked out the perfect stain to match the floors. They would need to attach hooks into the bare beams stretching overhead for the hanging plants she wanted, but those things gave her something to still look forward to.

It gave *them* something to do.

Together.

Some items on the table had tags attached. Others looked like they had been used. Vera suspected someone—probably Vaslav—had been playing in the dirt as a few pots were filled but nothing else.

Did he feel like he needed to wait?

She'd wanted this for him, too.

"He put your lilac thing—the one at your place in the city?—in the back, I guess," came the familiar voice of Kiril from behind Vera.

She didn't turn around to face Kiril, not wanting him to see her watery gaze while it took an inventory of everything around her. Maybe her tears came from the sudden swell of happiness at seeing one of her dreams come true, or it could have been the fact that the person she wanted to share it with was not there.

"Lucky I grabbed that for you the week before, huh?" Kiril asked.

Vera let out a slow breath that helped with the shakiness in her voice when she replied, "I hadn't really thought about the fact that it survived."

She didn't tell anyone, really, but Vera had needed to stop thinking about the bomb and her lost villa. Never mind the damage to her neighbors' homes on either side of hers, or the trauma to an otherwise quiet and safe community. She had to stop obsessing over an event she couldn't even remember that didn't entirely feel *real*.

Maybe once she saw the flattened space where her villa had once stood, that mindset of hers could change. For now, *not* thinking about it protected Vera in a way she couldn't explain to the rest of the world, but she wouldn't apologize for it, either. She had to do what she had to do to get from one day to the next.

"Oh, and the bench came in yesterday for it," Kiril added.

Vera spun around fast. "What bench?"

Leaning against the wall, Kiril shrugged. "The bench for the lilac in the back. Vas said he ordered it. I don't know."

Right.

Kiril only knew what he had been told, and Vera couldn't expect more from the kid. She didn't bother to explain her sudden desire to leave as she passed him by to head back down the stairs. Never mind that the bench he mentioned shouldn't even exist.

Technically.

Vera was supposed to pick one out. Yet another thing her husband had forgotten to mention in her time away that he apparently took control of and handled. Except with this, Vera wasn't entirely sure how she felt about it.

She'd yet to even see the bench.

Kiril followed behind Vera in silence, but he veered off downstairs to head for the kitchen when Mira called out his name. That was fine. Vera could find the bench all on her own know it was somewhere in the back of the house. She used Vaslav's den to exit onto the rear porch, and there it sat. Next to Irina's lilacs in bloom.

Backless and curved, the seat of the bench was carved from a single piece of wood. Where it sat on the ground only a few feet away from the porch's steps, Vera had a great view of the glossy wood and every grain and color that stretched from one side to the other. It was the cherub, chubby-cheeked with a head of curls and angel wings, branded into the middle of the seat that took her breath away.

Vera took the steps slowly, but she couldn't look away from the wings of the cherub that wrapped around the infant like it was holding the baby in a cradle. Depicted with closed eyes; eternally sleeping.

Once she was close enough, Vera traced the burned lines in the wood grain that were protected by the glossy finish on top. She asked Vaslav time and time again to let her come home, and his refusals always felt cold and hollow. A part of her thought it was because he didn't care that she wanted to be home with *him*, but now Vera wasn't sure if that was actually the case.

He went on like she was still here.

Never stopped thinking of her.

Like she didn't even leave.

"Mira said the food's ready. Did you want to eat out here?"

Vera had heard the sliding doors of Vaslav's den open, but the sleeping angel took all of her attention for the moment.

"I'll come inside," Vera called back.

Kiril didn't reply, but the door didn't slide shut, either.

"Where is he? When is he coming home?" she asked.

"He was here last night," Kiril said.

As if he had nothing else to offer—or he knew nothing else to tell her. Knowing Vaslav the way she did, and his strange relationships with the people around him, it wouldn't even surprise Vera for that to be the case.

Like normal.

Nothing had changed.

Oh, but it had.

"By the way," Kiril added while Vera buried her shaking hands into the front pocket of her oversized hoodie, "the Hummer's filled and your keys are by the door. If you want, we could visit Hannah."

The kid knew the right thing to say.

Vera spun on her heels like a toy top. "Can we?"

He nodded. "Yeah, but after dinner. Vas said I gotta follow the rules, or I can't stay in the house."

"What rules?"

"Mira's."

Mira had rules now?

Like the kid could read Vera's sarcastic thoughts in her expression, he explained, "Just for me—and I'm not allowed to miss a meal."

Ah.

Well …

Not all change was a bad thing.

"So, dinner first," Kiril said.

Vera smiled. "That sounds fair."

*

The hospital made an exception for Vera when she arrived terribly close to the end of visiting hours. As it were, the head nurse recognized Kiril, and even used his first name, so she seemed to understand that Vera being there was a big deal.

Maybe for the woman in the bed, too.

No matter how much Vera had wanted to be in Moscow just to be by Hannah's bedside over the past months, nothing really prepared her to see her friend unconscious and unmoving in a bed. A shell of herself, really.

Not entirely there.

It was all so strange.

Hannah didn't look physically injured which made the situation harder to wrap Vera's mind around when the nurse had urged her to talk before leaving. As if Hannah and Vera had so much to catch up on, and a lack of response shouldn't stop her from speaking.

Yeah, *strange*.

After taking the seat next to Hannah's bed, Vera decided to at least give the nurse's suggestion a shot. What could it hurt?

"Hey, Hannah," Vera whispered to her friend.

She didn't mean to speak so softly, but the second she was alone in her friend's private hospital room and the doors slid closed, there was no one to see her overwhelmed. It was a lot. From the prone redhead with her eyes taped shut in the bed to the many machines and monitors displaying numbers, graphs, and more things Vera couldn't understand.

Every shade on all the windows had been drawn. *She responds better when the room is dim*, explained the *midsestra* before she left Vera and Hannah alone.

Vera tried to shake off her nerves, and even cleared her throat to make sure whatever came out of her mouth next was louder and clearer for her friend.

Vera had slipped one of her hands alongside Hannah's, grabbing tightly around her fingers just in case her friend squeezed back. Hannah's other hand, attached to an IV line on the other side of the bed remained still and propped on the top of her midsection's swell.

"You're about twenty-four weeks today," Vera informed the quiet room.

Or it felt like it.

Despite the laundry list of information the nurse had gone over with Vera about comas and Hannah's current predicament—including all the possibilities and likelihoods—she wasn't sure that her friend could hear her. Besides, even if Hannah could hear her, it wasn't as if anything Vera had to say would make up for how they found themselves.

Especially *not* Hannah.

"Did they tell you yet that you're having a girl?" Vera asked.

Hannah gave no response.

More than anything, Vera wished that they had taken a few more minutes to discuss the future. Even a brief second to get out all of their *what ifs*. Did her friend have any names in mind? Did she want the baby to be Christened like she had been? *What do we do if you don't wake up?*

That question screamed at Vera, and the fact she didn't have any answer except the ones that felt selfish left her with guilt chewing on every last shred of her broken heart. What right did she have to want to promise Hannah she'd do anything and everything for her friend's child when Vera had barely wanted the baby that should have been her own?

The truth didn't just hurt.

It was bitter, too.

Like broken glass, unforgiving.

While she had been careful about the way she held Hannah's hand so that it remained touching her belly, Vera still felt the unborn baby shift and move inside her mother. Like a wave shifting from one side of the swollen sheet tucked around Hannah to the other; it was both amazing and sort of terrifying.

The hiss of air as the door seal broke and the panels slid open echoed in the quiet room. The *midsestra* from earlier—the one who had known Kiril by name and smiled wide at Vera's introduction—stepped into the room with a folded white blanket and pillow tucked around her arms.

"I brought these for you to have if you're staying. It's only me and another girl on the ward tonight, so we'll be quite busy," the woman informed.

"I don't think Kiril will want to hang around that lo—"

"It wouldn't be the first time that boy slept in the parking lot of this hospital. Trust me."

Vera gave the blanket and pillow a second look, considering.

The nurse shrugged, adding, "And the blanket was even in the warmer. Your chair lays flat like a small bed, by the way. There's a lever on the side to do it."

Her attention shifted back to Hannah.

Then, to the nurse again.

What reason did she have to go home?

No one would be there waiting.

"I'll stay," Vera told the woman.

21.

At night, Moscow was *most* beautiful—it really came alive, vibrant and practically breathing. In Vaslav's humble opinion, anyway. He'd never been very fond of the city to begin with, preferring the solitude and privacy his rural beginnings offered, so in one way or another, he always made his way back home to Dubna.

Or the general area.

When he did have to spend his days and evenings in Moscow, however, he enjoyed it most at night. So much so, that he'd been known as a brigadier—and later, boss—who didn't do business until the sun was down. Truthfully, he didn't really think men of his sort were meant to be out in the daylight and public like the rest of polite society.

Then, no one had to pretend.

They were all exactly what they were meant to be. He liked that.

"You're quiet," Igor said beside Vaslav.

Both men glanced upward in sync as the elevator they'd been riding in for the last three minutes finally chimed to announce they'd reached their floor. The mirrored panel doors, dirty and streaked with *something*, slid open to reveal the long hallway waiting for the men on the other side. Worn carpet and tattered wallpaper decorated the hall of doors all the way to the far end where a steel exit door had been propped open with a brick.

"I'm going to be honest and say I wasn't sure the elevator would make it to the top," Vaslav said as he stepped out of the elevator ahead of Igor.

"The shape of the building wasn't the reason they condemned it last month," Igor replied.

Vaslav eyed the number on an apartment door as he passed it by, noticing the crack that allowed him a small view inside the entrance of the run-down place. A coat still hung on a wall hook, but more concerning was the rodent shit crunching under his feet.

"Just how many rats?"

Igor sighed, several feet behind Vaslav, muttering, "Apparently, it was a bad infestation."

No shit.

The owner of the building likely ignored the pleas of his low income tenants, and it wasn't until something tragic happened that the building had been condemned. Wasn't that how the story was typically told?

"Lucky for us," Igor said, not quite caught up to Vaslav who neared the end of the long hall, "the city hasn't shut the power off yet, and a friend tipped me off on the way to get in when I mentioned needing something high in the area."

Vaslav nodded to himself. "Kiril, you mean. He's

been playing with locks again, has he?"

It wasn't surprising. The kid often traveled back and forth to the city; he had an entire social life that Vaslav didn't try to keep up with that existed outside of the time he spent in Dubna or working for Igor. Nobody could tell Vaslav any different, either.

"Well, at least he finally picked up a fucking call from me, no?" Igor punctuated the statement with a tight smile Vaslav caught when he glanced over his shoulder.

He had nothing to say to that—as Kiril and Igor's hot and cold relationship didn't make a whole lot of sense to Vaslav to begin with—so he offered his friend nothing in kind. Silence was far better than a polite lie.

Standing in the doorway where the light from the fire escape ladder led up to the roof, Vaslav breathed in the wet city air. Chillier at night, it rattled a bit deep in his lungs with every gulp. Once Igor caught up to Vaslav, he thrust the long case he'd been carrying toward Vaslav.

"Take it up—I can manage the ladder," Igor said.

It was a shame to say—and he never did because Igor's pride undoubtedly made the man aware—but Vaslav was usually a few steps ahead of his friend now more often than not.

Igor still had to learn how to breathe through his new pain. Damaged nerves from burns and shrapnel made every step a sacrifice and punishment, and brought with it a slight limp that softened some of Igor's looming gait. As far as Vaslav understood it, Igor fired the doctor who recommended he try a cane to take the weight off his bad leg.

The last thing the man needed was to be doing

anything at all except resting and medicating in the safety of his own home and bed, but their life afforded no reprieves.

Not that it mattered.

Igor made no complaints.

Frankly, at this point in time, he also didn't have the option to if he wanted to end any question of his power and control within the borders of Russia. If he staked his claim as the new boss, made his seat unquestionably clear, then Igor would have the time he needed to really heal and recuperate.

"Up we go, then," Vaslav grunted before stepping out on the rickety metal ledge protected by an equally rusty railing. He minded his hands for anything sharp that could leave him with a nick as he climbed the escape ladder with the gun case tossed over his shoulder. He had no plans for a tetanus shot after they were done tonight.

Just a long drive home to a beautiful woman he'd missed terribly. Both things would have been equally tortuous, but only one was actually worth the suffering.

Vaslav didn't offer his hand to Igor after he'd reached the roof, and his friend lingered on the top rungs like he needed an extra second or two to breathe. In fact, he figured Igor would want him to pretend like he didn't struggle at all, so that's what Vaslav tried to do.

Folding his arms over his chest, he squinted at the bright lights of Moscow staring back at him from nearly every angle. The darkness of the sky helped to dull some of the glow, but his skull still throbbed with his ever-present companion. The pain made him tired especially when the migraine had been chasing away any chance of a rest for days.

"It doesn't get easier, does it?" Igor asked after he'd finally climbed over the edge of the roof's cement wall.

Vaslav's shoulders tensed at the question, and what it implied. "The pain?"

"All of it."

"I don't think we share the same—"

"Pain is pain. There was a time you wouldn't get out of bed before a glass of vodka to wash down your Vicodin. I understand that better now."

A lump in Vaslav's throat kept him from warning Igor of playing that dangerous game but only because who was he to judge or give advice?

"You learn to manage it," Vaslav settled on saying while the wind picked up on the roof and carried away anything else he might want to say. Nothing about living, with or without constant pain, was particularly easy. Then, Vaslav nodded at the item he'd noticed despite the shadows. "Well, someone left you a chair up here to sit in and shake it off, anyway."

Igor soon found the chair in question, folded and propped against the building's air flow system. Caked with a layer of city dust, Igor didn't even bother to brush it off before he made himself a seat on the black cushion. His expression showed the relief he found when he wasn't standing and his back had something to rest against.

"Are you going to be able to hold the gun?" Vaslav asked as he dropped the gun case from his shoulder, and kneeled to the dirty roof to begin his work.

Igor scoffed. "Don't be offensive."

"It was an honest question, comrade."

"Yeah, well," his friend replied grumpily, "*don't.*"

Igor even scowled.

Vaslav chuckled, reminded of himself as he glanced up at an irritated Igor that barely even wanted to have a conversation anymore. That feeling was all too familiar for Vaslav, and the depression that could sometimes come with it took a strong will and mind to shake off.

And time.

Everything took time. From growing to dying.

Igor continued his contemplative silence while Vaslav constructed the long barrel rifle that had been a birthday gift not too long ago. He hadn't properly played with the weapon since the day Igor gave it to him, but putting together the pieces and snapping the scope into place was still a familiar puzzle he could have done with his eyes closed.

Guns were the only thing in Vaslav's life that he was convinced he would never be able to forget. No matter what his brain did to prove him differently. He clung to the way his muscles seemed to remember every weapon he'd ever touched. From butt to barrel, every groove and dip was a picture he could paint in his mind.

With the clip loaded and ready, Vaslav handed the rifle toward his friend but Igor didn't reach back. Too busy peering through a pair of mini binoculars to notice Vaslav and the gun ready for him, Igor sighed at whatever he found in the skyscraper in the new business development sector of the city that was five years in on a ten year plan for expansion. The partially developed block, however, rented office space like a revolving set of doors.

Anyone with a checkbook willing to sign a lease had access to the poorly secure building with only a handful of guards—all of who were willing to be bribed for an evening.

"At least tell me what you see, *suka*," Vaslav insulted.

Just to get Igor's attention.

It worked.

"Fuck you," he replied in kind, swiping one hand in Vaslav's general direction while never taking the binoculars away from his face.

"You know I hate when things have to be messy."

"What's messy?" Vaslav asked back.

"Nothing." Igor dropped the binoculars and met Vaslav's gaze before he deadpanned, "*Yet.*"

"*Da*, well, these things happen."

"They don't have to, actually."

Oh, no.

Vaslav disagreed, and he'd even take the time to make sure Igor understood why, too. "What did you see?"

Grinding his jaws until he'd worked through his thoughts or pain—either were possible—Igor snatched the rifle from Vaslav's outstretched hands without a word. He exchanged the gun for the binoculars, and instead of depending on Igor's description of the scene in a rented office space in the building across the way, Vaslav had his own perspective.

Of course, they'd picked the perfect time.

Not a blind in sight.

Every tall window, covering the floor to ceiling from one side of the conference room to the other, was open and illuminated to show the men gathered inside. Most sat around the long table meant for business associates and files, paperwork and laptops.

Certainly not the bags and stacks of dirty money piled in the center of the table.

Vaslav scanned some of the faces.

A few he knew.

Some, he'd even sat down with over the years and enjoyed a meal or otherwise. All had paid him millions upon millions of dollars to remain under his good graces and protection. And more importantly, he trusted none of them.

Not a single captain in his bratva could call themselves his friend, and Igor would do well to follow Vaslav's beaten path in that regard. The less friends a man had in an organization like theirs, the better prepared he was to deal with any and all situations.

Feelings rarely got in the way.

More interesting were the few men who had gathered closer to the head of the conference table. Their hands waved as wildly as their animated discussion that didn't seem entirely friendly. No doubt, discussing the situation at hand.

"All they're missing is their boss," Vaslav said.

Igor didn't respond to the comment.

A half hour ago, Igor should have walked inside that building. According to the information the men waiting across the way were concerned, their boss was a no-show, in hiding, owed money they could probably benefit from keeping, and now they had time to talk about it.

Again.

If they hadn't already discussed the state of their organization and boss above them, they wouldn't feel so comfortable to freely do so at the moment. Perhaps not all of them were bad seeds. Maybe only a few needed to go. *Any* would serve to teach the lesson Igor and Vaslav had planned tonight.

Like fish in a barrel, all they had to do was pick.

Eeny, meeny, miny, moe.

"I'm going to call in a couple of favors on some old friends," Igor informed. "I had a decent offer from Jersey."

Vaslav dropped the binoculars to glance down at his friend in the chair who winced as he shifted in his seat. "Mind the kick in that gun, yeah? It'll hurt your back ramming into that chair."

Igor didn't act like he heard Vaslav's warning.

Pride truly was a bitch.

"I think it'll be better to bring in people from the outside—even if they're loyal to a different man, at least decent money will keep them on task until I settle into this fucking seat," Igor muttered.

"It's not a bad idea," Vaslav conceded. "You know how I feel about the Americans, though."

"It's *Jersey*. Adrik—"

"Are we shooting or talking?" Vaslav interrupted.

Igor dead stared the building across the way while he balanced the rifle across his knees. "I can't wait until Vera gets back in the country, and I won't have to see your face but for once a fucking month. You're a lot more irritating to deal with when my entire back feels like it's still on fire, Vaslav."

That made Vaslav grin.

Little did Igor know …

"She's already home. Arrived this afternoon."

Vaslav would have liked to be in Dubna to greet his wife and start making up for that time they spent apart when she should have been enjoying her newly married life, but sometimes his priorities liked to shift.

He figured she'd be jet lagged and sleeping well into the early morning hours, anyway, so it gave Vaslav lots of time to help Igor finish out his business before returning where he belonged.

Igor let out a chuff. "I should have known."

That Vaslav would get his wife back on home soil the very second he knew his plans with Igor would fall into place? Perhaps, Igor should have assumed as much, but Vaslav wouldn't fault the man for being distracted by other things.

Vaslav nodded at the gun, repeating, "Talking or shooting, huh?"

"My bet's on three before they're all under the table or out of the room," Igor said, and readjusted the rifle so his gaze stared down the scope.

"Kills?"

"Kills, murders. It's all the same."

Right, right.

"Fucking messy," Vaslav agreed.

22.

"Wake up. We're home."

Vera blinked more than a few times before she remembered where she was and who that voice belonged to. In the driver's seat of the Hummer, Kiril was already yanking the keys out of the ignition and had his seatbelt unbuckled.

Actually, she couldn't remember him buckling it at all if he even did when they left the hospital earlier in the morning.

"I swear, the second I turned the engine over, you were out," Kiril said to Vera as she yawned and stretched until her back cracked in the passenger seat. "I knew you were tired."

Vera tried to roll her eyes, but it was a half-assed effort. Nothing he said was a lie, anyway. When he strolled into Hannah's hospital room just after breakfast had been served saying it was time to go home, Vera couldn't find a reason to argue.

Other than the obvious.

Just because she desperately wanted to stay by Hannah's side, whispering to her friend and the unborn baby also listening to all the secrets told between them, didn't mean she reasonably could. The promise of a familiar bed called to her in a way she couldn't refuse.

Vera still wore the sweats and hoodie that she'd flown home in. Jet lag was a real thing that, even after a solid night's sleep and a nap on the two-hour drive home, nothing helped but time and rest. Even so, Vera still had to convince herself to leave because what good could she do for her friend when she was tired and practically useless because of it?

"I did get some sleep," Vera told Kiril. "And the nurses didn't even wake me up until the shift change in the morning, so it was a good stretch."

Kiril cocked a brow in disbelief. "On those hospital chairs? Yeah, right."

"Mine reclined."

"It's not any better."

Well, he wasn't wrong.

"Maybe my back hurts a little," she admitted.

Not that Vera wanted to complain. She didn't have any standing to do so compared to her comatose, pregnant friend she'd left behind—*alone*—in the city.

Eyeing her companion in the unmoving vehicle, who didn't make a move to open his own door, Vera wasn't quite ready to exit just yet. A part of her was waiting for the stiffness in her back and legs to ease up as the rest of her body woke up, but the other side of her had already noticed the black Hummer parked next to theirs in the circular section of drive in front of the house.

Vas was home.

All the days that had passed since she last spoke to her husband now felt like a wall she had to climb over for some unknown reason. It wasn't even that many days, just four since he called to say he'd chartered her a jet, but it seemed like more.

Vaslav had a way of stopping her entire world right in its tracks, and she didn't get any say in the matter. Sending her away wasn't all that different from bringing her home when it meant it would be done on his timeline, and how he demanded while Vera was left to deal with the emotional whiplash and unanswered questions that wouldn't leave her alone because of his choices.

Constantly.

"You look like a deer in the headlamps," Kiril noted.

Were her thoughts written on her face?

Vera sighed, not able to take her gaze from the vehicle beside theirs. "Sometimes, the people you love will make you angry, Kiril."

The teen's nose crinkled at the idea. "Can't say I know much about that—*love*, I mean."

She thought he probably did, but his love was still a shallow thing. Fickle and easily ruined, but also overflowing and fast to grow.

He was still young.

There were also those who had never been loved in the way they should be—instead, their love was toxic and poison. Love was something they had to relearn.

"You've got time," Vera muttered heavily, finally unbuckling her seatbelt and straightening up in the seat. Her gaze traveled over the front of the house until it eventually came to land on the steps, and then up to the door. It remained shut tight. "But they will.

The people you love will make you angry, and maybe they won't feel bad about it, but it helps to remember that even the anger you feel comes from your own place of love. Be gracious, give grace, and be forgiving, okay? Especially to the people you love. Even when they make it hard. You never know when you're going to wake up and they're not beside you anymore."

Kiril cleared his throat, and scooped up his handful of personal items—a wallet, lighter, and pack of cigarettes—from the middle console. "I guess I'll keep it in mind?"

Vera glanced back at the house, but her thoughts remained focused on the man somewhere inside waiting for her. At least, she hoped he was. "Yeah, we all need to."

That's why she'd said it out loud.

She also needed the reminder.

*

"Are you sleeping?" Vera asked.

"*Trying.*"

The grunted reply—made more muffled by the quilt wrapped around Vaslav as his back faced his den, and he remained turned into the couch—still had Vera smiling. Mira, who had been removing any wilted roses and feeding the ones in larger vases by the stairs, was the one to direct Vera to the back of the house when she asked about Vaslav earlier.

Who knew where Kiril was?

The kid made himself scarce.

Vaslav, on the other hand, wasn't hard to find at all. Vera only needed to notice the dark den, pulled shades, and lack of coals in the fireplace to know why she found her husband curled on the sofa, hiding from the rest of the house.

Chronic pain meant just that—constant.

All the time.

Without fail.

The question should never be *if* Vaslav was in pain, but rather, how much. She'd once thought his migraines came and went like waves, but she'd only recently factored in how she never considered that they didn't leave. He hid it well, or perhaps his pain management skills had sharpened over the years so that he seemed unfettered by the minor troubles. Or her lack of understanding might have come from the fact that Vaslav would rather be in pain and staring at her, than hiding his face in a pillow.

Except he was doing that now.

She didn't need to make Vaslav's suffering worse by engaging in frivolous conversation or questions about how he was feeling—or *had been* since she was gone—when the answer was obvious. Nothing really changed.

Even if their world was a little different.

"I'm …" Vera struggled to find the right words— the reunion she'd desperately wanted with her husband had been saturated by her bitterness and anger until faced with the reality.

Lamely, because she couldn't form a sentence that didn't begin with something hurtful or equally vicious, Vera slapped a hand to the side of her thigh and said, "I'm really tired. I guess I'll go up to bed."

If he wanted to find her, then he could.

Vera turned away from the sofa at the same time she heard the cushions squeak with Vaslav's slow roll.

"Where are you going?" he asked, confused.

Vera didn't face him as she fiddled with her fingernails, ignoring the urge to pick at them some more. "The roses are beautiful."

Vaslav cleared his throat. "I overdid it. The smell was—"

"I loved them."

She wouldn't say it if it wasn't true. Vaslav had never been the one between them that appreciated a lie. Her interruption seemed to silence any other complaints he might have about the hundreds of roses she'd arrived home to the day before.

"You could have chosen red, or pink—a rainbow of colors even," Vera said, shrugging. "No, you picked white."

The color one usually picked to express condolences for someone's loss and sorrow. Vaslav didn't acknowledge the suggestion Vera's words pointed to but that wasn't a surprise. With him, his actions always spoke louder than anything he ever said.

Or didn't, for that matter.

"And I saw the bench," Vera added. "It's beautiful, too."

"Do you have a spot in mind?" he asked

Not particularly. Other things weighed there. He was high on the list amongst everything else making a mess in her mind and heart.

Vera saw Vaslav's hand reaching for her, but she didn't move as his fingers skimmed over her wrist. It was only once he'd tugged her hands apart, and his fingers locked around hers that she turned slightly. Half facing him, but still prepared to leave. Not that she really wanted to go—the tender strokes of his thumb against the side of her hand drew a wet, shaky breath from Vera.

"Do you want to sleep upstairs?" she asked him. "It's better than this couch."

"I don't like being up there without you."

"You never told me that."

Vaslav's shoulders rolled with a lazy shrug while he watched her through one squinted eye. "It's not the same without you."

She wasn't used to Vaslav being so frank when it came to his feelings, and in that moment, it hit Vera like a ton of bricks. She did her best to change the subject if only to keep her own swelling emotions at bay.

"The contractor did a gr—"

"And my mother is also up there now so I can't even get beyond the first landing of steps," Vaslav interrupted before Vera could start in on the studio and greenroom upstairs.

She blinked at what he implied. "Right *now*?"

His dry chuckle sounded hollow. "Ah, I said that wrong. Her ashes. They're up there."

"Your mother is dea—"

"On a dresser," he continued like she hadn't spoke as his gaze narrowed with whatever he envisioned right in front of his face. "*In a bag.* I stopped going up to get my clothes after Mira told me she'd put them up there after the crematorium sent it with a courier to the house. We're back to Mira getting things together for me. I don't know where to put the bitch, but she can't stay up there."

Jesus.

It took all but a few sentences for Vaslav to make it clear to Vera how his life could also fall apart around him without her near.

"You don't have to do anything with the ashes, and I'm sure Mira and I could figure something out," Vera said, her words seeming to ease the sudden rise and fall of Vaslav's chest. "You could have told me your mother had passed away when I was in New York. Why didn't you?"

He swiped a large palm down his dark beard. It, too, had thickened and lengthened with growth he would probably want to shave soon.

"They had to move her to a palliative unit a month ago—she lasted a week in there. You sat on the same couch I did when the shrink said her body couldn't keep doing what she was doing to it. I hear the staff at Roseville kept her company. What did it matter if I told you? I never wanted you to know her to begin with."

And now she never would.

Between them, the unspoken sadness hung like a heavy cloud. She suppressed the urge to apologize about his mother's passing because he wouldn't want her to waste the breath.

"Vera, come here."

It wasn't a question.

He punctuated the demand with a tug of her arm that jerked Vera closer to the sofa, and him. Her knees hit the floor as he rolled to his side, and reached for her again. This time, those roughened hands of his held her face.

Like fine China.

Precious, and his.

His first kisses were tender. Like his thumbs that swiped away the traitorous tears every time they dared to fall with her blinks. Vera didn't want to cry, or be sad.

She'd already done a lot of that.

Just without him.

I missed you.

He let her cry more and apologize for the many short, terse phone calls between them even though she really wasn't all that sorry. She did regret the wasted time because she knew they didn't have nearly enough as it was.

I love you.

She unfurled his quilt and climbed into the small spot on the couch where more of her body hung off the cushion than what remained on it, but he didn't let her fall. Wrapped in the blanket, up to her neck, with him, tight in his arms with her head against his chest where she could hear his heartbeat …

Vera could breathe again.

She breathed *better.*

It was as if they had been one breath before forever when time stood still. When a choice was taken from her; when her entire life turned upside down. She didn't expect anyone to apologize for those things.

Nobody said life was fair, but he let her cry about it all the same. About their time apart; poor Hannah; even how she came home to a house without him. She got it all out while his fingertips and stare studied and adored her the same way he always did when he held her close. Until her tears ran dry, and her trembling soothed to nothing but shivers because of his hands. He didn't apologize for any of it, but that's not what Vera wanted from him anyway.

She needed this.

Them.

Together.

Vaslav's fingertips drifted up and down Vera's spine under her hoodie. "It's a new year. A new spring, *kisska*. Anything can happen. Anything could change."

With him—*at least*, she told herself—she wanted to believe it.

EPILOGUE

Three months later ...

"*There's definitely something wrong. They're taking the baby tonight.*"

Nine words.

Two sentences.

Vaslav didn't particularly enjoy eating his words, but the universe seemed determined to make him do exactly that. Everything did change.

It had been three weeks since time stopped, and he watched his wife walk out their front doors with empty arms and a worried smile.

He didn't tell Vera not to leave.

Every phone call she made that filled him in on the unnamed baby girl's achievements in the NICU ward left Vaslav feeling like he knew a child that he hadn't even seen before.

Vera wore that same worried smile—even if it was tired, too—when he opened the front door after hearing Mira shout from her rooms on the third floor that they were finally home.

They, she'd said.

Specifically.

That should have been Vaslav's first clue.

Vaslav had known who it was before Mira announced it because of Marrow's sharp barks of warning from the rear of the house when he heard the vehicle rumbling up the winding drive. Had it been an unknown vehicle, the dog would have made a beeline for the front and kept barking all the while. Instead, his noise remained at the rear.

He didn't expect to see the infant car seat hanging from his wife's elbow, but that worried, tired smile of hers never faltered as she walked closer to the steps. Vaslav couldn't see what waited beyond the black shade pulled high on the car seat, but the bundle of pink blankets were more than visible.

"Hannah's mother is flying in," Vera said, breaking the silence between them first.

Vaslav blinked, and forced his gaze up to meet hers, and she climbed the steps toward him. "I tried to warn you."

Or maybe *prepare* would be a better word for the caution tape Vaslav had needed to proverbially put between Vera and her still comatose friend in the recent weeks since the cesarian birth of Hannah's infant. He thought it unfortunate that Vera didn't have the extra months with Hannah pregnant to keep her safe from her mother's melding and control in her medical care, but they had already walked on very thin ice doing what they had.

It was time to step back.

"Once the baby was born, Igor had practically no

control over how Hannah's medical care would be handled. Her mother can—"

Vera's furious gaze darted from him and down to the bundle in the car seat. "The baby's been born for three weeks, and she never even asked about her!"

Vera's sudden rise in tone earned a tiny squall from the car seat. Like the jaws of a dog had snapped at his ass, Vaslav jumped at the new noise, not even trying to hide the glare he shot in the general direction of the dangling car seat.

"Stop it," Vera scolded him. "Don't you want to look at her?"

A part of him did.

Another part of him wanted to drive across Moscow where he would find Igor—well-protected, sure, but what did that matter—and drag him to Dubna so *he* could take care of his child. No sacrifice could be made without some caveats, of course.

This was certainly one of those.

"They're very small," he told Vera.

She blinked up at him. "*What?*"

"Babies," Vaslav explained. "And this one is extra small, no? She was born early, they gave her those steroids for her lungs, and—"

"Vaslav, what is the problem? We talked about this. Igor goes nowhere without his security. He doesn't even sleep in the same place for more than a week. And wasn't it you that told me he wasn't in any shape to be caring for a newborn last week?"

They had talked about this.

This very, exact thing.

Many times.

The entire damn situation was so inevitable, in fact, that Vaslav didn't think there was any way around

Vera caring for Hannah's child. The woman's mother wanted nothing to do with the baby; the father wasn't in any shape to be one; and Vera couldn't help but martyr herself every goddamn chance she could.

Inevitable.

"Fine," Vaslav muttered as he heard the footsteps approaching the front door.

Kiril and Mira, likely.

Coming to greet the baby.

When did Vaslav ask for a full house?

"Fine, what?" Vera asked him.

"Let me see her."

The demand made his wife beam. She didn't wait for him to say it a second time before spinning the car seat around and pushing back the rounded shade. He kneeled as Vera placed the car seat to the stone, getting a better look at the hazy, blinking eyes of the wrinkly baby snuggled under a pink blanket. The cotton cap with a big bow in the front fell over the baby's eyes when she yawned.

Vaslav reached in to fix the hat, only to be frozen when the baby's blinking gaze seemed to finally focus on him. "Hello there."

She *was* small. Too tiny even if she could eat on her own and didn't seem to have any other troubles besides underdeveloped lungs that just needed time and occasionally medication.

Vera bent down beside Vaslav, fixing the blanket around the baby and then stroking the tiny fingers grasping onto the edge of the fabric. "She likes to be rocked to sleep, but she won't take a dummy at all."

"A dummy?"

"Those soother things," Mira said where she had to stand with Kiril in the doorway.

Vaslav nodded over his shoulder at her like he understood, but he really had no fucking clue. A baby was so out of his element. This entire situation felt un-fucking-real to him.

The baby yawned again, startling Vaslav just like the first time. Even if there was no noise to her sleepiness.

"She's not going to bite you," Vera said.

Yes, she would.

Eventually, the damn things got teeth.

Vaslav sighed, pulling the blanket away from the baby so he could access the car seat's safety buckles.

"Well, what's her name?" Kiril asked, finally jumping in on the conversation.

"What are you doing?" Vera asked Vaslav.

"Picking her up. I need to get the fuck over it. You know—*just do it.*" Vaslav fumbled twice with the five-point harness before Vera swatted his hands away to do it for him. Clicking the connectors apart seemed incredibly easy for her.

Had she practiced?

"There, you can pick her up now," Vera said. "Support her head and back."

The baby *fit* in both his hands. The zippered sleeper—pink like her blanket and hat—swallowed the girl in fabric. He'd picked up rocks heavier than the child. Vas would be a liar if he said that fact didn't scare him even more.

How did people keep little humans alive?

At least, the baby stopped wiggling when he rocked her against his chest. Except there he could smell the lotion and baby powder that seemed to soak into his lungs with every breath. After a few seconds of him doing that and staring over the front yard, it wasn't so bad.

"She doesn't have a name," Vera said, answering the question that had hung in the air since Kiril asked it. "Igor didn't want to name her."

Vaslav reached for Vera's hand, and squeezed.

She shrugged. "He had a hard time even looking at her. I think it's just—"

"We'll pick one," Vaslav interjected, stopping that worry of Vera's in its tracks. "We'll figure out something for her. She can't be nameless."

"Yeah, okay," she muttered with a nod.

*

His dick was testament to his wife's innate ability to turn him on without even needing to try. While a migraine played the drums between his ears, his cock would still get hard with Vera straddling him. She'd only climbed into the bath with him to do that thing he liked with her fingers on his scalp, but he was *weak*.

Well, she did get in naked.

On top of him.

Practically *ready*.

His favorite sex—perhaps not his best, though—was when he had to do very little work. She did the heavy lifting on top, getting herself off how and when she wanted, while he enjoyed the show she gave him.

The hot, bubbly water was a plus.

Vera sealed the deal when she laid herself over his chest, and worked her hips in slow circles against his dick. She smelled of the strawberry scented bubbles he'd poured into the bath water and she tasted of her need with every hungry kiss she stole from him.

Those whines crawled out of her chest.

Higher and higher.

Between her kisses, she begged for what was left of him.

"Won't you come in me?"

Until both his hands clamped onto her ass, and held her into him, as she squirmed and squealed her way through an orgasm that milked out the beginnings of his own. He still needed to be deep in her when he came; hugged by her body; smothered in her life.

As soon as the rush of endorphins and pleasure started to fade from Vaslav's nervous system, he was still left breathless from his lingering pain.

"Fuck," he groaned, his head falling back to the ledge of the tub.

With his eyes squeezed shut to ward off the worst of the returning pain, his wife's fingers helped to ease his breaths as they scraped and scratched along his wet scalp.

"If only I could keep you coming for—"

The high-pitch wail of a baby sent Vaslav's eyes flying wide open. He found his wife staring back with a sympathetic smile as her hands retreated from his scalp.

One week in with a newborn.

Too many more to go.

"You good?" she asked as she steadied herself in the tub to stand, and leave.

"For now," he replied.

He'd have to be.

"Ava," Vaslav said to Vera's back as she wrapped her body in the silk robe she'd discarded earlier.

At the random name, she looked over her shoulder. "I like that."

Shocker.

She'd not cared any for the other ones he'd picked out up until that moment.

"It's a palindrome. Like her mother's."

Spelled the same way front and back.

Also, Russian.

Igor had ignored Vaslav's calls all week.

He tried not to think too hard about that.

"Ava," Vera repeated to herself.

In the tub, Vaslav stretched out again, and let his arms hang over the rounded edge. For once, his wife didn't bitch about the droplets of water falling from his hands to the floor in a gathering puddle she'd probably step in later.

He wasn't good at remembering to clean it up.

The baby cried again.

"I'm coming, Ava," Vera called to the infant in the next room.

She even slept beside their bed.

In a tiny bassinet.

His wife tossed him a wink before she exited the en suite bathroom. She didn't ask for his help, but the longer he listened to her soothe and chat with the baby girl—who probably wanted a diaper change and feeding as it was nearing in on her typical two-hour mark—the less he wanted to stay in the bath.

So, he didn't.

Vaslav let the tub drain while he dried off. Keeping the towel snug around his waist, he leaned in the doorway to watch Vera as she sat in the rocking chair he'd put in the corner for her. Complete with a rocking stool, it made feeding the baby easier and more comfortable at night.

Mira made bottles ahead.

Vera kept them cold in their mini fridge.

Vaslav had been the one to figure out the trick of letting hot water from the sink tap run over the bottle to warm the milk to lukewarm in mere minutes. It saved them more time than running downstairs to heat water for the same purpose.

He'd warm this bottle, too.

Like all the last.

First, he just enjoyed the sight of her like she was— whispering sweet nothings to a baby that had practically no one except the woman holding her in her arms. They were worthy arms, though, and capable of the most amazing things. Vaslav was the proof.

Ava would be in good hands.

Well, until her mother could finally hold her.

ABOUT THE AUTHOR

The author of too many novels to count, Bethany-Kris is a
Canadian, lover of much, and mother to four sons, a
glaring of cats, and a pack of dogs. A small town in
Eastern Canada where she was born and raised is where
she has always called home. With her boys under her feet,
a snuggling cat, barking dogs, and a spouse calling over his
shoulder, she is nearly always writing something ... when
she can find the time.

Find where to follow BK and keep up to date with all her
book news at www.bethanykris.com.

OTHER BOOKS

The Beast of Moscow Saga

The Beast of Moscow
The Lies Between Lovers
The Beauty Who Loved Him
The Breath Before Forever

The Darkest Lies Trilogy

The Agreement
The Promise
The Marriage

After Another Trilogy

One Step After Another
One Breath After Another
One Second After Another

Boykov Bratva

Fractured Ties
Essence of Fear

The Guzzi Legacy

Corrado
Alessio
Chris
Beni
Bene
Marcus
The Firsts: A Guzzi Legacy Companion Novel
The Guzzi Legacy: Vol 1
The Guzzi Legacy: Vol 2

Renzo + Lucia

Privilege
Harbor
Contempt
Forever
Cusp
Renzo + Lucia: The Complete Trilogy

Andino + Haven

Duty
Vow
One Last Time
Andino + Haven: The Complete Duet

John + Siena

Loyalty
Disgrace
John + Siena: The Complete Duet
John + Siena: Extended

Cross + Catherine

Always
Revere
Unruly
The Companion
Naz & Roz

Guzzi Duet

Unraveled, Book One
Entangled, Book Two
Cara & Gian: The Complete Duet

DeLuca Duet

Waste of Worth: Part One
Worth of Waste: Part Two

Standalone Titles

Pink
Pretty Lies
Dirty Pool
Effortless
Inflict
Cozen
Captivated
Dishonored

Donati Bloodlines

Thin Lies
Thin Lines
Thin Lives
Behind the Bloodlines
The Complete Trilogy

Filthy Marcellos

Antony
Lucian
Giovanni
Dante
Legacy
A Very Marcello Christmas
The Complete Collection

Seasons of Betrayal

Where the Sun Hides
Where the Snow Falls
Where the Wind Whispers
Seasons: The Complete Seasons of Betrayal Series

Gun Moll Trilogy

Gun Moll
Gangster Moll
Madame Moll

The Chicago War

Deathless & Divided
Reckless & Ruined
Scarless & Sacred
Breathless & Bloodstained
The Complete Series
Maldives & Mistletoe

The Russian Guns

The Arrangement
The Life
The Score
Demyan & Ana
Shattered
The Jersey Vignettes

FANTASY ROMANCE

The Hunted: A 9INE REALMS Novel

Find more on Bethany-Kris's website at
www.bethanykris.com.